Nothing More Than A Puppet

M.J. MOON

Published by M.J. MOON, 2024.

NOTHING MORE THAN A PUPPET

First edition. June 11, 2024.

Written by M.J. MOON.

Also by M.J. MOON

Nothing More Than A Puppet

To my beloved husband, Mr. Moon,

You are the light that guides me through every chapter of life's adventure. Your love and unwavering support have inspired this story and filled its pages with warmth and depth. Thank you for being my rock, my confidant, and my greatest love. This book is dedicated to you, with all my heart.

Forever yours,

M.J.MOON

Nothing
More
Than A Puppet

Chapter 1: Pages from The Past

Amanda's eyes peeled at the dark ceiling of the apartment bedroom. Outside, she could hear faint engines of cars, horns, and sirens of machinery. New York was a place that never sleeps, just like Amanda. She couldn't possibly let her eyes drift into a cozy dream; something was just pulling her awake, but she couldn't place the reason. She then twiddles the ring on her left hand, resting on the finger connected to her heart, round and round in circles. She grazed her fingers over the beautiful jewel diamond, looking at the ceiling. Amanda then felt a slight shuffle beside her as she looked over to the side and saw Jacob sleeping peacefully, showing his little grin. Amanda smiled at Jacob and thought how lucky she was to be married to such a sweet man and has been for a while now. Everything was great. She moved her head upwards, again looking at the ceiling above. But something was bothering her. Amanda stroked her cold hand over her shoulder and felt her stitched scar. The stitching where Amanda got stabbed. Her mind then flicked through the memories of the school shooting, the blood, the kidnapping, the drugging, and of course. The one and only Bailey. That name made her feel sick inside. It turned her stomach into multiple knots. She wanted to forget it. But she couldn't. The memories were burnt into her head. She was physically hurt, starved, and mentally abused all because she wanted Jacob. She was one crazy bitch. Amanda shook her head and slowly slipped the covers off her, pulling her legs out and placing her two feet on the cold floor quietly. She glanced behind and saw Jacob was still sleeping peacefully. She went into the bathroom and clicked on the light, which made her wince. She adjusted her dilated, dull eyes and greeted her reflection. Her face looked rather pale, and her eyes looked tired. She tucked her jet-black hair behind one ear and stroked her face in distress, continuing to stare at her flesh in disappointment. Amanda then stood tall, pulled her shirt slowly down at her shoulder, and turned her body to the side. Her scar glared at her with painful thoughts, and Amanda couldn't peel her eyes away. She then lifted her t-shirt and looked at her stomach for no reason. She just looked at it in disgust and remembered how skinny she was when she was starved. Amanda grazed her cold hand over her stomach, sucking in and pinching at her skin. That's until she noticed something began to wrap around her waist, covering her hand. Amanda slowly pulled her eyes up and looked in the mirror. Behind her stood Bailey, her face was dark, and she had a crooked smile. Amanda's heart dropped meters deep, and her eyes widened. Her breath quickened, coming in shallow gasps as her adrenaline spiked, sending her body into a flight-or-fight mode. Without fully processing the situation, she screamed loudly, her voice raw with terror.

In a desperate attempt to protect herself, Amanda instinctively spun around and threw her hand up in defense. Her body moved faster than her mind, driven by the primal urge to survive. But her voice was a rather manly scream, "AGHH. AMES! IT'S ME!" Amanda then saw Jacob standing tall and clenching his face. "Jacob!? Oh god! I'm so sorry I-" "It's fine! It's fine. I was just checking on why you are up so late," he said, stroking his face. "Jacob, I'm sorry! You just freaked me out." "Who else would it be!?" he shrieked. "Why are you up so late?" "I couldn't sleep..." Amanda nervously said, looking away in the other direction. "Oh right, okay. So that's why you are so jumpy and punched me?" Jacob said sarcastically, folding his arms. Amanda leaned against the sink and looked down at the floor. She was afraid to repeat her name and admit her thoughts. She didn't want to remind Jacob at all.

"It's nothing..." Amanda said. "Ames, talk to me." "Babe, it's okay. Just something was on my mind," she continued, walking back into the bedroom as Jacob followed. "And what was on your mind?" Amanda then sat on the edge of the bed and glanced at the floor for a while. She then looked up at her husband, who stood tall over her with his arms folded. But she didn't want to say her name. Things were going so well between her and Jacob. She didn't want to wreck their minds even though hers wasn't so stable. "I was just worried that we slept in for work," she lied. "I guess I'm just tired. Maybe I had coffee too late," she shrugged. Jacob then placed himself next to Amanda on the edge of the bed and wrapped his arm around her as she naturally rested her head on his broad shoulder. "Well..." Jacob said, turning his head and looking at the clock. "It's only half one in the morning. You have plenty of time to still get rest." Amanda then let out a small, short, soft laugh and finished it with a quiet sigh. Jacob looked down at his wife and noticed how rather upset she looked. "How about in the morning I make breakfast? Sound good?" "Last time you made breakfast, you set the eggs on fire, Jacob." "Oh yeah," he chuckled, remembering the moment. She then yawned and stretched her arms, letting out a cold shiver. Jacob then smirked and tucked some of Amanda's hair behind her ear. "You sure you okay though?" "Humph. Just the coffee ticking over." "Alright, then, if you can go a day without coffee," he said, picking her up bridal style and placing her onto her side of the bed, "Then I will buy you a whole new batch of dividers. Sound good?" "Jacob, you broke." "Okies. Night!" He said, immediately jumping onto his side of the bed, making it shake, and as quickly as ever, switching off the light. "Night..." Once again, the room went dark, and Amanda looked up at the ceiling where the night sky glowed a faint crystal blue. It's okay... I'll never see her.

Amanda slowly paced up the school hallway, holding her gun up high. She darted her eyes in every direction, taking slow, careful steps. She then moved her hand to the left of her shoulder and pressed down on the radio button that sat on her vest. "Jacob, do you copy?" she whispered as the static sound echoed down the hall. There was no response. She then held down the button again. "Jacob? Do you copy?" Amanda released the button, waiting for an answer, but still nothing. She decided not to think about it, knowing that Jacob was fine. She then came round a corner to find another empty hallway that was so dark and gloomy. The only thing she heard was her slow, uneasy breathing through her nose. She kept her hands still up high with her gun at aim. Her heart was racing. Her nerves were shaking out of control; anything could happen. Anything at all... That's until Amanda suddenly heard a rattle from a small closet door. She jumped to the sound and spun her body around, still having her gun aimed right at the oak brown door. She stopped, just glaring at it. Her mind was going through many questions that made her tremble even more.

Amanda placed her right foot forward first, then the left, gradually luring closer to the door. She then stretched out her arm, grabbing out for the handle. Her hand touched the gold metal object, and she took a deep breath. She then, as quickly as ever, pulled down the handle. But everything happened too quickly. Suddenly, a man dressed in all black pounced forward and dug a sharp knife into her shoulder. Amanda was startled and screamed in pain, dropping her gun that slid on the floor. Amanda pulled out the knife that was now cuddled into her flesh and felt her warm blood trickle out. She groaned in agony and lifted her head, which she was then immediately grabbed and thrown onto the floor like a ball. Her body smacked onto the polished floor, and she again yelped in pain, holding onto her shoulder where she could now feel the blood on her hand. She couldn't take a second to help herself as his strength was too strong, and everything was happening too quickly. She placed her hands on the floor and tried to get up, but a sudden force pulled her back down, making her smack her head. The unidentified man grabbed her two wrists and slammed them onto the ground.

Amanda kicked and screamed, trying to escape, but he wasn't budging. He then suddenly pierced a needle into the skin of her arm and forced the liquid inside her bloodstream. Amanda looked down and saw an opportunity, an open area. She then lifted her right leg, kicking the attacker right in the crotch. It immediately made him quiver and fall sidewards, groaning and groping his area. She then rushed to her feet to run away and find Jacob. But when she stood up standing, everything began to spin. She couldn't focus her eyes as they became blurry by the minute. She felt her body crash into the lockers that echoed down the halls, but the sounds kept looping in her head. Her body then switched off, falling onto the floor like a doll, and her eyes became dark. But it then felt like seconds when she finally opened her eyes to a horrific sight. "Hello, Amanda." Suddenly, Amanda jumped forward, gasping for air, grabbing her chest, and breathing heavily as if it looked like she was on a mile run. She felt warm and sticky with sweat. She glanced her eyes around and saw that she was in her room. The morning awoke as the sunlight crept through the small cracks of the long-draped curtains. It was just all a dream, a flashback. A bad Memory. She turned her head and saw Jacob's side of their empty bed and saw the red glow of the alarm clock that read 8:03 a.m. Amanda pulled her covers off her in a panic of not wanting to be late for work, as she is always there before 9. She rushed into the bathroom and looked at her face, covered in sweat of fear. She rubbed her eyes in grief and tried to forget about it. Amanda grabbed her 100% cotton towel and turned on the shower. She placed her two feet in and let the water soak her thoughts and worries away. She ran her hands through her hair, lifting her head and letting the water hit her face. She then moved her hands onto her shoulder, again accidentally grazing her fingers over her scar. It immediately made her jump and look behind her, thinking of Bailey. But she saw nothing other than the steamed, empty room. Ever since the whole thought of seeing her last night and the dream has traumatized her. Amanda switched the warm shower off and stepped outside, wrapping her body around her soft creme towel. She walked back into her room, grabbing her hair and squeezing the damp water out of her soft, dark black hair as water droplets dripped onto the floor. She opened the doors to her neatly organized cupboard, picking out her classic pantsuit outfit with a blue shirt. Amanda opened the bedroom door, still drying her hair with a towel, and walked out to see Jacob in the living room eating a bowl of fruit loops. "Oh, morning!" He smiled with a mouth full of colorful cereal. "Sleep well?" Amanda just fakery smiled and walked into the kitchen. "Yeah, great." "You sure?" he said, pulling himself up and going to the kitchen. "You were shuffling a lot in your sleep," he said, setting his empty bowl on the counter. Amanda pulled out a mug and flipped the kettle on. "No, honestly. I'm fine. I slept amazingly," she said, turning her body to Jacob. She then looked at his face and noticed a bruise on the side of his eye. "Omg, did I do that!? Jacob, I'm so sorry-" "Ames." Jacob then placed his hands on her waist. "It's fine." Amanda then sighed, looking at him. She wanted to tell him what happened last night, but she didn't want to hurt him again or bring him back to those memories. They were happy, and Amanda didn't want to ruin that. "All right." she said softly. "But you got to get ready for work. I'm not going to be late," Amanda finished, kissing his lips and immediately returning to the bedroom. "Ames?" Jacob shouted after her. "Humph?" she stopped, turning her body round and looking at Jacob. "You know you can talk to me, right?" She then paused, just looking deep into his sorrowful eyes. Small guilt began to rise, but she couldn't just tell him. She couldn't tell anyone. Bailey was dead in their memories. "Yeah. Of course," But just not Amanda's...

Chapter 2: Down for It

Jacob sat in the driver's seat, pacing down the overcrowded bunked-up road as the traffic flowed slowly. Buildings whizzed past, and the sounds of horns echoed in the distance. People leaned out of their car windows, yelling and even some were just glaring at the red traffic light as they came to a stop. Amanda, on the passenger seat next to Jacob, rested her head against the palm of her hand where her elbow rested on the side of the door. She kept her eyes peeled outside her window, watching New York be the classic animal town it is. Ahead, she watched small kids cross the road with oversized school bags. Some walked beside their mum and Dad, and others held onto both hands, picking up their tiny legs, and got swung in the air as they giggled and kicked their feet in excitement, begging for another round. Amanda created a small smile and admired their family bond. It was something that always broke a lost smile for her. The red glow of the light turned green, and the force of the car pushed Amanda back ever so slightly. She then turned to the side of the window and looked at the sea of vehicles. There were many colors, yet yellow stood out the most—the classic yellow cab. Suddenly, something black blocked her vision, covering many cars, but it wasn't too close. A person on a motorbike with a thick black helmet was blocking her sight like a dull rain cloud. They wore all black, just like Terry, but it wasn't her, as blonde curled hair poked out in the back of their helmet and rested softly on their leather jacket. It was clear it was a female biker. Amanda continued to stare at the biker as something fell off. She didn't know what it was, but she just knew something was up, as a weird feeling started to rise in her very subtly. She tried to ignore it and decided to face her head forward, looking away and peeling her eyes at the slow traffic. But in the corner of her eye, she could still see her dark black motorcycle, still riding at the same pace as her. She couldn't help but draw her eyes back at her. But just then, she felt uneasy as the biker's head was turned in her direction, and the black helmet revealed a faint reflection of Amanda. She didn't know if she needed something or why she was looking at her, but she could feel her eyes burning into hers behind the helmet. Just then, slowly, the blonde biker lifted her hand off one of the bike handles and brought it up towards her eye guard, and Amanda's eyes followed. Suddenly, in one flick, the guard pushed up, revealing something she would never forget, not even those eyes. These were the eyes that no one else had. It was like a rare gem. Cause it only belonged to one person. Bailey. At that moment, Amanda did nothing but just freeze in shock, breathing heavily. She didn't know what to do or even if she was real. Indeed, she was just seeing things again, right? She decided to look the other way and squinted her eyes shut, trying to wipe away her so-called false seeing. But when her eyes opened, those same blue eyes kept looking at her with such an evil smug glare. That's when Amanda knew that she had to be accurate. The feeling of fear kept climbing in her chest, and it gradually got worse as they both stopped at a red light, just having a stare down. Jacob, tapping his fingers on the wheel to the faint song on the radio, noticed how quiet Amanda had been and ripped his eyes away from the road. He saw her head turned, just looking out of the window. Yet something didn't feel right about her ever since last night. He looked down and noticed her chest rising quite fast, like something was scaring her. Amanda just stared at her like a deer froze at the stop of headlights. She slowly moved her hand to the car handle and placed her fingertips on top, not moving her eyes an inch. Jacob noticed her movements and felt unsure of what she was doing. "Ames, you, okay? You seem-" Just like that, Bailey gave Amanda one grinning wink of an eye. Amanda couldn't possibly take another chance to be with her again. Jacob's words were cut off as she immediately slammed her knee into the compartment in front, making it fall open and reveal an armed pistol. Amanda swung the car door as quickly as ever and aimed the weapon at her.

"NYPD, HANDS UP AND ON THE FLOOR!" she shouted. Surprisingly, she seemed somewhat startled and did her commands, turning her bike off, setting it to a stand, and holding her hands up high. "Amanda!!? what are you-" "Turn around and hands where I can see them!!!!" Again, she abodes by her wants and slowly turns around with her hands still up high. Amanda placed her gun down and grabbed her arm, pushing it upwards against her back and slamming her body onto her car, making a low, muffled bang. She then began to take off her helmet, twisting and pulling. "I never want to see your face ever-" Amanda got cut off by Jacob grabbing her arm and spinning her around. "What are you doing!?" "What do you mean, what am I doing?" she mocked. "Just take a look at who it is!" But just then, when Amanda turned back around, she had never felt so ashamed. A crash of fear, embarrassment, and confusion hit her like bricks. Her heart dropped to her feet, and she quietly gasped. It wasn't Bailey. It was just another typical biker blonde, looking as scared and confused as Amanda. Her eyes weren't blue but were a wild forest green. Her face was not the features of the person she thought it was. It wasn't her. It was just another vision, another mind game. "But...I-she-" Amanda stuttered. "Amanda, what is going on with you?" Jacob said in a soft, concerned tone. She just looked around her. Behind Jacob, she saw people standing outside their cars in shock while others remained inside. Amanda then immediately spun around and gently pulled the blonde off the vehicle. "Ma'am, I am truly sorry. It was all a misunderstanding. I-"Save it, cop! I don't have time for your shit," she said, pulling her arm away from Amanda and setting back on her bike. Jacob then stepped forward, holding his badge. "I'm Detective Peralta of the NYPD. If you would like to come back to the nine-nine, I'm sure we can-" "I'm not here to learn names. Save your breath," she spoke, punching her engine on and driving off. Jacob then turned around and saw everyone standing about, looking at Amanda. "All right, people, the show is over. Please return to your cars," he shouted, and everyone slowly did their commands, and one by one, each car drove off. Amanda placed herself back into the passenger seat of the car and watched everyone's eyes look at her as they were driving past. More and more, she felt ashamed. She, as a cop, has never embarrassed herself like that before. Yet those eyes looked so real. She thought she was real. But her mind was playing tricks once again. I am losing my mind...

The elevator doors slid open on the bottom floor, and Jacob and Amanda stepped in. They both looked forward, and Amanda pressed the button. Not one word was said about the rest of the car journey or even inside the elevator as they walked in. Amanda was so ashamed she couldn't even look at Jacob. But how can she tell him? How can she tell anyone? They will all think she is too crazy for Jacob to disown her. She wouldn't want that. Neither would Jacob. Who would ever want a crazy wife or a friend? She couldn't possibly let anyone know. But she was just overthinking everything. 'Amanda, are you honestly okay-" "I don't want to talk about it, Jacob," she replied bitterly. "Oh...cool, that's fine." The doors finally opened, and everyone was there. Something Amanda wasn't used to as she was always there early. But, this time, she was 20 minutes late. She didn't make eye contact with anyone and instantly placed her bag down on the floor and sat down at her neat desk. Just in front, Jacob slammed himself on his chair, slumping down and swirling around, but also looking at Amanda as she immediately buried her face into a case file that was recently sitting at her desk. "So, Santiago, you are twenty minutes late. Did you forget to lift your favorite pen again?" Terry laughed, sitting at her assigned desk across the room. Amanda glared at her and sighed, slamming the paper file shut and leaving the bullpen as her heels clacked to every step. Jacob sat uptight and watched her storm out of the room and looked at Terry with squinty eyes. "What? was it something I said?" she said in a monotone voice. "No..." He paused. "It's fine, I just have to talk to her." He pushed his body off his chair and made his way in the direction Amanda went. Everything seemed strange, yet she wouldn't tell him what was wrong. That's all he wanted to know. Jacob then learned that she made her way up to the rooftop, but not just any rooftop, their rooftop. It's a place Amanda hasn't been for a long time... Something was bothering her, Yet Jacob didn't have a clue. Not even one thought about it being about Bailey. His mind erased that name. But why couldn't Amanda?

"**P**risoner 84. You've got company..." The metal doors clattered open, echoing down the gloomy prison walls. The pace of the prisoner's feet banged with the chains dragging along the floor, and the one on their wrists swung side to side. The keys on the officer's uniform, hooked and linked onto his belt, rattled as he escorted prisoner 84 to the visitor center, where a wall split the room, dividing the trapped criminals and the innocent free civilians into two groups. A large plastic window sat in the middle, like every other small window that was numbered, with one old rusty chair. Each side had blinding walls for privacy and even had a rather old torn-away phone on the left on the white-shaded fence, where it was a point of communication. This was the closest you would ever get to the outside world of contact. This was life in prison. "Window number 4," the officer said, pointing. "Your company is sitting there. Again, there will be no point in banging on the window or shouting. Understand?" "Clearly..." The officer nodded and escorted the prisoner to the chair. They then sat down, making the chains rattle, lifted the cold black phone, and so did the person in front. "Long time no see, Tay." the visitor spoke. "Hum, you've grown, brother." "Indeed," he smirked. "Now... " he said, leaning closer to the window, "Let us talk business...Amanda, isn't it?"

Chapter 3: Let's Talk Business

Amanda slammed the door open, greeting her eyes upon their rooftop, Jacob and hers. So much rage and confusion pulsed through her body like a circuit. But those daring blue eyes seemed so natural to her, yet her mind played cute tricks. Maybe she was losing the plot... Every step she took closer to the bench, facing towards the beaming sun. Her heart is crushed every time. With every step, those eyes kept switching from blue to green. Every step. Blue. Green. She finally sat herself down on the sky-watching bench and covered her face with her cold hands. So many emotions, and Amanda couldn't handle it. She had no idea what was wrong with her. Her head felt like a ticking bomb, ready to go off at any moment. "God," she sighs. "I'm losing my mind," Amanda mumbles as she strokes her face in distress. Her shoulders felt heavy, and her chest felt compelled by many rocks pressing down on her. He was dragging her down. Amanda lifted her head, letting her skin soak in the heated, warm summer glow and breathing calmly. She opened her eyes, squinting to know the golden sun's rays would blind her. But it didn't... Something light, floating softly in the wind, was shadowing her eyes. She followed her eyes on the object, watching it move closer to her and softly graze on the concrete and stopping at her shoes. Paper. The paper lay on the ground, softly lifting to the wind, nudging her at her feet. It was like it was taunting her to lift it. But something didn't feel right again. Yet her confusion and curiosity overtook her body, and she reached for the paper. Amanda picked up one of the corners and flipped the sheet. On the other side, it made her freeze. This began to unlock past sayings and memories of that gruesome room and captivated her mind. It wasn't plain paper but a photo she once held. A picture of Jacob and Bailey. Right on top of the roof, exactly where she was. Kissing. *"Pfft, that's funny. I could've sworn I saw your pal too busy kissing someone else rather than saving your pity ass"* *"See. He doesn't give a shit. How else did you end up here? They don't care."* *"Oh, please. Do you think he deserves some nerd? Like, come on! Look at you! I wouldn't even think you were a cop."* "Amanda." She jumped when she heard her name, blinking twice. Then, once again, the sheet of paper she once held was gone. "Ames?" the voice called again. She turned her head and saw Jacob approaching her with small steps. "Knew you would've been up here," he said, pulling up the legs of his trousers upwards and sitting next to her. But Amanda just gave a quick, short laugh. She was looking down at her hands. She then investigated the distance, where building tops peeked over. She sighed and looked at Jacob, gazing at the world ahead. Amanda then cleared her throat. "Jacob?" "Hmph?" he replied. She then took a deep breath and looked right into his brown oak eyes and a sharp glance down. "Do ... Do you-" she then looked at him, pausing. She wanted to tell him about Bailey, yet she was too scared of what he would think of her. Would he even have a clue what she was going to say?

"What's up..." he said, turning his body to her side. "Do you think I am crazy?" she lied. Knowing well, that's not what she wanted to say. "Is this about earlier?" he said with a more sorrowful tone. "Perhaps..." "Well then, no, of course, I don't think you're crazy. You've just had a rough week, and whatever you say was a mistake. It happens, Ames." "Yeah..." she nervously laughed. "Just saw something. That's all." "What did you see?" Amanda then froze, not knowing what to say. "Uhm. I-eel. Saw." she stuttered, glancing to the right. "A knife! Yes! A knife...Hehe. No lies here, bro." "Oh, thank god. I thought you were going to say you saw a ghost or something," Jacob said, waving his hands." then I was going to think you were going a bit cuckoo," he finished, making a face and waving his finger in a circular motion at his head. "HAHA." she yelled in the fakest laugh." Well! Glad I did not see Casper the ghost! Is it cold out here? It's cold out here! Wanna go inside? Let's go inside!" she said, as quickly as ever, pouncing to her feet. But she was stopped by Jacob's grip over her wrist. "Like I said, you know I'm here to talk. Right?" Amanda then smiled, turned her body, and grabbed his other hand. "Of course." She then wrapped her arms around his neck, gazing into his eyes. He then creased his signature smile and placed his lips onto her small ones. "We better get going inside though, or captain will have a static fit." she broke. "yip"

"Detective, and Sargeant Santiago. You late," said Holt, in his low monotone average voice. "Care to explain?" "I... Um," Amanda stuttered. "I slept in. Again. Sorry, sir." Jacob intervened, saving her innocence. "Not a surprise, Peralta. Surely you do know what alarms are for?" "PFMT...of course, I know." he scoffed. "I only get up to your alarm. I have no clue how to set mine up," he said, leaning over and whispering beside Amanda. "Good. Then use it. Don't let it happen again," Holt replied, returning to his office. "Got it, Dad!" Jacob then turned and sighed, "God, I need to stop doing that." "Yeah. You've got real Daddy issues..." "Title of your sex tape, anyways! I'll catch you in a moment. Me and I have a case file to catch up on. Later," Amanda lifted her hand slightly and waved. She settled herself onto her old work desk right next to her and started logging on but heard a sudden slam next to her desk.

"Oh. Hey Terry." Amanda replied in a questioning tone. "You are not in your uniform..." "Oh. Yeah, this," she said, pointing at her casual business wear. "The uniformed squad is doing the paintball test at the tactical village. I did insist on going to help them out as a sergeant. But Officer Jennings-" "That Gary guy?" "Yep." "Ugh," she rolled her eyes in disgust. "I know... Anyways! He insisted I have a 'Day off,'" she quoted. "That man doesn't know Me. What psychopath takes a 'Day off'!? " She air mentioned again. "But I didn't want to get into an argument, as it would be like fighting with my reflection... So, I decided to take his word and, well, wear the old style of Amanda Santiago." she showed. "Cool, dope. But that's not what I came over for," she said drastically. "Oh. It isn't-" "No. What was wrong with you this morning? You seemed all weird and jumpy." "Me? Weird? Push, no, bro... It's all good, light and breezy," she said, tucking a piece of her black hair behind one ear. "You touch your hair when you are lying. Tell Me what is wrong." Amanda sighed and looked the other way. She glanced around the room, seeing everybody doing their own thing as usual, and landed her eyes back down at Terry. She wanted to tell her, and she was like her sister. Maybe she could trust her... "Okay, okay... But promise me you won't tell this to Jacob?" she said, lowering her tone. "Sure, of course." Amanda sighed, looked down, and processed what she would say. "I keep seeing her." she then looked up. "Seeing who?" Terry asked. "Bailey." When Terry heard those words, her grip tightened, and she tensed her teeth together. "No matter where I go, I see her. I falsely arrested some blonde biker this morning, thinking it was her. It's like those blue eyes follow me everywhere. I can't sleep anymore. My mind is always ticking over my thoughts. I feel like somehow, I'm still under her control... " "So that's why you were late?" Amanda just shook her head slowly. It felt good to tell someone. But she felt like she was talking like a person with a mental health condition. "I know. It sounds crazy, I am crazy-" Amanda said but got cut off by Terry's voiceover topping hers. "Amanda, not once did I think you were crazy. I don't blame you for seeing these illusions." Terry stressed, "What happened to you will be traumatic. But it's going to be fine. Just remember, that bitch is behind bars, and it doesn't matter when she is going to get out. Cause everyone around you? We've got your back. You are safe." "Thanks, Terry." Amanda smiled softly, feeling slightly better. "No problem. Anyways. I must call Ashley. She wants a session where I call her beautiful every five minutes. But again. It doesn't matter when she is going to get out. You are safe." Terry then got up and walked away from Amanda. Hearing her heels become more distant. Yet her advice was sweet, but something she said did startle Amanda and got her thinking. When does she get real...?

"Yes. My name is Amanda Santiago. I've said this over a thousand times over the phone, idiot," Bailey glared. "You would look prettier if you didn't look so dead inside," said her brother. She was smugly laying back on his chair. "Keep that attitude up. I will show what dead looks like; now listen up," she snapped. "All right, all right..." He laughed, now sitting up front. "Just get to the plan already." Bailey licked her teeth and glanced at her eyes, left and right. She then pulled the phone closer to her mouth and talked in a low, deep tone. "Her name is Amanda Santiago. Her partner is Jacob Peralta. They are both detectives from the NYPD." "Ooh, detectives. This will be fun..." "Oh, trust me. They are easy to play. This shouldn't be hard for you," Bailey grinned. "I want you to at least go undercover as a former journalist." "A journalist?" he scoffed. "What am I, a Nerd?" "Bingo!" she smiled. "That weak little rat craves over Nerds, typically one herself, and this is why it's the perfect plan," she smirked, leaning closer to the window. "I want you to break them, Jason. Be interested in her work, do whatever to grab her attention, I don't care. Just take her out places and gather the details. I'm sure it will make poor wee Jacoby jealous..." "What about you?" Jason replied. "Don't worry about me. As soon as I'm out of here..." Bailey laughed. "They have no idea what's coming..."

Chapter 4: The Dark Shade

"All right, all right," Jason spoke into the phone. "This is all fun and games with talking and planning. But what am I getting out of this? Cause I don't claim things without a reward, Irvine." Bailey didn't reply instantly. She smoothly glanced around the room, observing her surroundings before she dared to open her lips. " I knew you would've been greedy." she stressed through her teeth." Yes, of course, there is something for you. I was wondering if you were up for the task... " "Did I stutter?" Bailey then creased a grin. Her revenge was finally going to be back on track. Just as you think someone learns from their mistakes, you thought wrong. For her, it wasn't a mistake. It was a lesson from the beginning. "Those words have a deal, brother." Bailey then whipped her head behind her and looked at the ticking clock. "Listen in, I don't have much time. In the abandoned Mental asylum up North, bottom floor, Room 7. Thirty grand sits within the floorboards. That is yours. No one else's, understand?" "Loud and clear." "And I repeat," she leaned in, "Don't get caught." Jason continued to nod his head softly in glee and agreement. "You have yourself a deal, Tay." "Times up, number 84. Say goodbye to your friend." said one of the officers, approaching Bailey as his brown boots hit the floor in a shallow slap and placed his hand on her shoulder. She kept her eyes on her brother before leaving and spoke one last time. "I need her. Don't fuck it up," she said, rising to her chained feet. She took one last look at him before she was yanked back into her prison life behind bars. "I Won't disappoint..." Jason grinned.

"Hey, Amanda, I-" Called Terry, approaching Amanda at her desk on the bottom floor, where all the uniformed officers were swarming. But just as Terry called out her name, she suddenly shut her laptop and looked at Terry with a nervous smile. "Oh, it's Terry! Hey girl..." "Hey, girl? Since when you have said that?" Terry said in disgust, "I've always said it." Terry then crossed her arms and tilted her head to the side, lifting one of her brows and glaring. "Whatever, Terry!" Amanda yelled in worry. Terry then rolled her eyes and sat herself down next to her second base, well-organized desk and slapped a case file onto her desk. "What's this?" Amanda asked, looking at the orange-brown paper. "Well, what does it look like? A case file, of course. I was coming down here to ask if you would like to work a case, like old times. But got rudely interrupted by your weirdness." "I'm not acting weird... You the one that's weird around here." "Sure," Terry replied in her monotone manner. "So. Want to work the case or not? Or is whatever you are hiding in your laptop more important?" Amanda glanced at her Apple Mac and looked back at Terry, who had a chill manner, arms crossed, and was slumped back on her chair. She then opened the file and looked inside to see it was empty. Nothing was in it, bar a couple of 20-dollar notes. "Terry, there is nothing in this. Where are all the filing papers? It's just money," Amanda said in confusion. "I've noticed you've been too stressed lately. So, I'm deciding to take you out, and "she paused," I don't know... Just get something."

"Oh, Terry, you really don't have-" "Yes or no." "Well... I mean, I am not doing anything, so-" "Okay, let's go then." "Oh- oh, okay then," Amanda said, pouncing to her feet and following Terry behind

Jason drove up the hill, listening to the faint crackling radio. His hands gripped the wheel tightly, smiling at the thought of the piles

of green he would receive. He turned a sharp left as the car tires scraped against the small stones on the road and was greeted by the old, rusty, unsettling Mental asylum. At the front, musty old stains were ringed around the missing letters, and the grey concrete collected layers of greenery. Jason smiled and parked his car outside the front doors, currently blocked with two wooden planks. Just then, he picked up a small black flashlight sitting on the side of his driver's seat and lifted a black duffle bag sitting across from him. He swung the black door open to his car and slapped the bag over his shoulder, slamming the door shut and striding his way to the front. He pressed the hollow button on the torch, which awoke the light. He pressed his face against the small window of cold glass, shining the stream of light down the dark, empty hallways, and hurried his eyes around, not finding anything. He then clicked the torch off and touched one of the planks, shaking it slightly. The double doors shook along with his pull and weren't nudging open. He smugly laughed, turned his body in a half-turn, and walked back to his car. He reached for his boot and opened it in a small red box. Jason set the empty bag down, along with his light, and clicked open the lid, opening the package, revealing it to be a toolbox. He lifted out a steel hammer, tossing it in the air and catching it with the handle, and laughed. He pushed the box to the back of the boot, lifted his things, and approached the double doors again, whistling a cheerful tune. Jason flipped the hammer around to the claw and positioned it on one of the nails that were smuggled in with the wood. He began to pull, and in one yank, the steel nail flung right out, bouncing onto the concrete. It finally allowed Jason to rip the rest with his bare hands, as the wood was now useless and no longer a barrier. Just then, he placed his two hands on the plank and pulled, making the wood snap in half. He then did the same to the other plank resting behind and grabbing his hammer and using the claw to pull out the nails. It wasn't long till the barrier was broken, and the double doors were now open. He stood at the entrance and just looked down at the pitch-black hallway. Nothing was to be seen. Not even an inch of detail. He again swung the black bag onto his shoulder and awoke his light. He began to walk down the aisle of abandonment, swaying his light from side to side. He pointed it at a rope lying on the floor as he began to walk past it, looking at it. "No. I'm coming with you. I'm going to leave Bailey here. Pass me that rope there." Amanda hobbled her way towards the rope and chucked it at him. He then threw Bailey on the floor and tied her to the nearest rusty radiator. He pulled the rope so tight he saw her hands becoming purple. "This is too fucking tight," she yelped. Jason then turned to a corner, piercing his flashlight first, and came to another, yet different, hallway. He then walked down a bit more and investigated one room where it looked like a changing room. He then placed his flashlight on-to the floor, where there was a puddle of stained red blood.

"Ames!? Ames!!?" said Jacob, shaking her violently by the shoul-ders. Amanda gave no response. "Jacob, she is losing blood!!" But it's nothing he hasn't seen before... Jason shrugged his shoulders and began his search for room 7. More and more doors began to appear, yet there were no numbers on them. That's until he was deeper in. Turning a cor-ner to a sea of doors, left and right. All numbered. At yet, his eyes im-mediately set on the number 7. Jason then smiled and made a quick sprint to the door and opened the metal door as it began to painful-ly creak and echo down the halls. He walked into the dark room care-fully, shining his light onto many objects, such as a rusty bed. But on the ground, something caught his eye. He knelt on one knee and saw what was ripped paper. He flipped it over and picked up the two pieces, putting them side by side. "Bailey?" he whispered in confusion, as it seemed to be a printed picture of his sister and her kissing someone... The black figure picked up the picture and stuck it to the wall for her to see and made his way out. "Enjoy your stay here. It's going to be a while." He closed the door shut, locking it from the outside. Amanda got up and ripped the picture in half. Jason placed it into his pocket and went fully onto his knees. He then grazed his hands onto the floorboards and started knocking. He continued to crawl, just knocking until his knock hit something hollow. He placed his ear closer to the floor and knocked again. "Bingo," he grinned. He then picked up his trusty hammer again and started slamming onto the floor. The wood began to splinter and break, revealing a cash of green. His smile increased even more, and his pace began to speed up. He then dropped the hammer, placed his hands into the hole, and grabbed his prize. "Amanda Santiago," he paused, smelling the money in pleasure. "You better be fucking ready...."

"So, what do you want?" asked Terry, now currently standing in line with Amanda in a modern coffee shop. "Hmm. I don't know... I-" "Oh, come on, Amanda. You took an hour deciding on where to go for coffee, so don't dare take an hour deciding on what type of coffee you want." "Well, what are you getting?" Amanda asked, also folding her arms and glancing at her friend. "Black. Like I always do." "Fine. Okay. I'll have the same." "Fine," she replied, stomping her way to the cashier and immediately opening her mouth. "Two black coffees, keep the change," she said, throwing a ten-dollar note. She then spun back to Amanda, who looked rather worried. Her face seemed rather dull and white. Her eyes kept locked onto the ground, and her hands rested on her hips. "Amanda, you, okay? You don't seem too good," Terry asked. Amanda then shot her head up and looked at Terry. She pushed out a small smile and shook her head. "Yeah. No fine. I just, um." she paused, placing her hand over her eyes. "I just need to go to the bathroom. I'll be back. Just," she said, now making a move to the bathroom but in a quick, rushed way. "Find a seat!!!" Terry stood still and looked at her friend, who was currently rushing to the bathroom. Amanda slammed the bathroom door open, seeing a current person at the sink, blonde hair, washing her hands. Not looking at her. But she didn't care. Amanda instantly crashed herself into one of the stalls and fell to her knees. A sudden sickness arose in her stomach and made her gag. She pulled back her hair and coughed into the toilet, throwing up and gagging. Her body was shaking, but thankfully, it didn't last long. She pulled her arm up and flushed the chain, resting her body on the door in exhaustion. She ripped off a piece of paper and cleaned around her mouth, pulling herself up to her feet, and opened the cubical door again to the blonde lady who continued to wash her hands. Amanda looked at her reflection and saw that her eyes were bloodshot and glossy. Her face was slowly creeping back to her normal color, and her shaking was calming down. She pinched her eyes in disparity and sighed. "Poor Ames..." a voice echoed. Amanda then lifted her head and looked to the left of her, seeing that the female blonde was still washing her hands, with her hair covering her face. "Pardon?" Amanda stuttered. "Feeling down, Amanda?" she spoke again. And at that moment. She knew that voice. Of course, it was Bailey. But, of course, it was in her head. "Go away. You are not real..." "Feeling scared, Amanda?" she spoke again, lifting her head now and looking into the mirror at her own reflection. "No... No, it's all in my head," Amanda replied, shutting her eyes and walking backward. "Feeling confused, Amanda?" Bailey hummed, cracking her head to Amanda. "It's in my head. It's in my head," She repeated. "But Amanda?" his voice echoes. "ITS IN MY HEAD, ITS IN MY HEAD!!" But a sudden tightness gripped around her throat. Her head smacked onto the wall, making her grunt in pain, and Amanda's eyes flung open. Greeting her blue eyes. "Three more days, Ames. Don't be too comfy." "YOU ARE NOT REAL!" Amanda screamed, closing her eyes, and fell to the floor. "Amanda!???" Terry called, now standing at the bathroom door, looking down at her friend cradled on the floor. Amanda opened her eyes immediately, picked herself up, and ran out the door. Pushing Terry back onto the wall and out the doors. Terry then looked out at the window where she ran. She looked so scared and confused. She then glanced her eyes onto the floor and reflected on what happened, to then remembered Amanda saying who she had been seeing these past few days. This time, it seemed to be getting out of hand. Terry only considered one thing that needed to be done. She then dug her hand into her pocket and opened one of her phone icons. Placing it to her ear. "Jacob... We need to talk."

Chapter 5: Scared

A manda stumbled out of the coffee shop door and almost tripped over her own feet. She didn't hesitate about where to go next and immediately ran to the left. So many daring eyes, all different colors, followed her movements. As she kept running, people parted out of the way for her, like a split end. Be she couldn't care. She was running. She ran home so fast that the tail end of her blazer caught in the wind, and her hair blew and swayed like a flag at a high stride. She wasn't being chased. Nor was she running after someone. She ran away from fear, from her delusional mind. Although she couldn't outrun her thoughts, like always, Bailey's taunting words looped in her head, making Amanda run faster, like she could escape the sound. "Three more days." You may not know what that necessarily means, but Amanda knew. She knew exactly what those snake words meant. Three days, just like what she read on her Apple Mac, right on Bailey's criminality data file. The words that were slammed to a shut before Terry's appearance, the words of how many days till she was released. Her breathing became heavier, and she could feel the heat rise to her cheeks. She continued to run in the dark streets, slapping her feet. It then became painful for her to run in heeled boots, but Amanda blocked out the pain. Only running was set on her mind. Running, running home- "Fuck!!!!" screamed a voice, tied in with the sudden sound of a liquid splash. "Are you blind!!?" shouted a man, who had a cap on that shadowed his face. His tone was a sour growl as he sucked in the air in pain while his black coffee soaked in his grey shirt under his black bomber jacket, steaming in the heat. But Amanda was too wrapped up in her own thoughts to even say sorry, as she would usually do as a good person. But she didn't dare to stop running. Home was probably the only place where she felt sustained and safe. Her mind was dedicated to being home, running past New York's finest cafes, food stalls, bookstores, and, of course, the weary public that made New York, well, New York. But they all began to distance themselves and open to her own avenue to home. Amanda skidded across the pavement like a cartoon character and ran up the steps, burying her hand into her Balzer and fumbling out her apartment keys, unlocking the door. Her heels clacked up the stairs that bounced around the walls like a tennis ball and came to a stop as she halted at her apartment door. Panting. she burst into her home, slamming the door behind her. Amanda then placed her back on her pink door and slid down, curling her knees to her chest. Her apartment was dead silent, dark too. She had never been home this early from work. It was only 9:30 at night, yet it felt later. She continued to sit on the floor, head down rested on her knees, breathing, catching her breath. The dark, empty house reminded her of old times when Jacob wasn't a part of her life. The thought sent a chill down her spine. She then lifted her head, now to see a strange ghostly vision of herself. Crying, her past self, on the floor crying. Just right next to her. Amanda remembered that day; she remembered that pain and hurt. She remembered Jacob yelling at her face. "Amanda, I don't want to get in a fight, but I'll stand my guard saying that I do believe it wasn't her. You're the person, out of everyone, who has been acting strange lately! You're also the person who has a smoking addiction! Plus, I couldn't help but notice that you've been looking at Bailey recently... Starring constantly... Like some freak!!" All because of Bailey. Purposely made her drunk to lose her job, but he believed her innocent lie. Jacob blamed it on Amanda. After those words, she remembered going home, resting on the floor, crying, just like what she was doing now, except blooming tears.

She continued to watch her vision-self cry, still curled in the exact position she was in, and wail. Amanda then watched herself lift her head and stand up, still sniffling and sobbing. She knew exactly what she was going to do because, of course, it was well remembered, and she stood at her feet. Amanda's past-self walked over to one of her shelves, in the corner near the dining table, where she had a photo resting in a beautiful silver frame of her and Jacob, the day they beat the vulture, and what Jacob would say. Amanda looked like a devil dog due to the tear gas and showed them both holding up a fully signed confession. "No... don't," Amanda spoke, knowing fine rightly what her past self was going to do. She then watched herself throw the picture onto the wall next to her, ducking down. The frame shattered into pieces, falling onto the floor. "Amanda?" She then turned her body round to see Jacob at the door holding the handle. He then flicked on the light that brightened the room. "Jacob? what are you doing at home?" "I could ask the same," he said, closing the door behind him. "What were you looking at?" Amanda then turned her head to see the broken photo that was on the floor, perfectly fine, sitting on the shelf with a new frame. Plus, her vision self was gone. "Nothing, um-just," She laughed through her nose. "Nothing." "Oh," Jacob nodded, pursing his lips together tightly, and walked over closer to his wife, resting one hand on one of the wooden dining chairs and inhaling. "So, Terry called about-" "Oh," she nervously laughed. "That? PSHH, I just didn't feel great in the bathroom. It's nothing I-" "No, Amanda," he paused, looking down, "I know about Bailey."

"**A**re you blind!!?" Jason shouted as his warm black coffee burned his flesh under his grey shirt. He looked up to see a young woman dressed in business attire looking at him with a frightful look. But he knew that face, The face of Amanda Santiago. He then watched her run down the street. But why? Jason then looked around him.

Some eyes glanced at him, and some carried on with their business. He then pulled his eyes back onto Amanda. Still frantically running down the dark, glowed street. Probably running home. That would be helpful to him. "Taxi," he then called at the yellow cab strolling down the cluttered road. The car parked right next to him on the curb and squeaked to a stop. Jason then threw his empty coffee cup to the side and jumped in. "Follow that girl," he pointed, seeing her become more and more distant. But the taxi driver didn't move. Instead, he just gave him an unsettled, confuddled look. "She is my sister," he stalled. " We are playing a fun game of chase. Gotta win." Jason laughed. The driver then made a small chuckle himself and nodded, following Amanda down the street, not driving too fast. The car drove past many of New York's finest cafes, food stalls, and bookstores. But then entered a new homey avenue. Jason kept his eyes peeled on his possession, stupidly leading him to her apartment. That's right, his control. His goal. His want. "Thanks. You can just stop here," Jason said, directing him to the pavement across from Amanda's apartment. "All right, sir, that's Four dollars and Fifty-two cents." He croaked in his smoker, raspy voice.

Jason pulled out his wallet, flicking through only part of his green that he claimed not long ago, and pulled out a crinkled five-dollar note. "You can keep the change," He said, pulling the grubby door handle forward and leaping out. "Hey," The driver called, leaning towards the passenger window. Jason didn't reply to his response but just discreetly turned his body around, placed his hands into his black coat pockets, leaned over, and smiled. "Good luck with your game! Have fun!" The old jolly driver said, so oblivious to the absolute truth. But he laughed at himself and looked down onto the floor, still having his hands in his pockets. "Thanks." He paused, "I will." The driver gave him a warm smile before driving off down the road. Jason shook his head in laughter and turned his body around, darting his eyes onto the building and began approaching it. But suddenly, he came to a halt. A white iced Audi, with bright headlights on like heaven entrance, pulled up next to the steps. Jason then hid behind a stiffly parked car across from the building. He then watched the light flick off, hearing a shallow click of a door opening. Just then, two pairs of rough sneakers, one shoelace was undone, flapping freely, and the other, in a loose bow, stepped out. His hair was an oak brown, slightly had a natural curl, and his eyes seemed rather dark from Jason's view. He watched the man skip the few steps with his leather jacket, layered with a hoodie underneath and a checkered shirt, up to the door and lifted out keys that shuffled down the street. Just when Jason thought the man was going to step inside, Jason stood tall to his feet but had to drop once again very quickly, as the young brown-haired male spun his body around like a clock and glanced his head left and right like he knew someone was watching him. Someone like Jason. He kept his body close to the parked car and still peaked his head, observing his every movement. But suddenly, something caught his eye. He was just hanging, swinging from the man's neck. A golden police badge, showing so freely. Of course, a police officer. Now, what was Copper doing at her apartment? Unless. He wasn't any police officer, he wasn't wearing their assigned uniform, nor did he arrive in a cop car. Plus, why else would he be here? A lover, maybe? No. A husband. Of course, the ring on his finger. He was just any guy. He then pulled out the ripped paper he found in the abandoned asylum. He was Detective Jacob Peralta. Husband to Detective Amanda Santiago. This was just too easy for him. He laughed in his joy, enduring how stupidly well-planned and structured everything was going for him. He then saw Jacob finally enter the building, and he had to act quickly, or he could lose him and never find out what door they swarm in. Jason stretched to his feet and softly ran across the road. He was trying not to place so much weight onto his feet to cause such a slap. He watched the door become closer and closer to its closing destination. But he wedged his foot in time, which negatively made a horrendous squeak. Jason pushed his cap down further onto his face and squinted. But to his hearing, it seemed like he didn't notice, as he opened his eye and saw the tail end of his shoe going up the stairs. He sighed in relief and carefully walked in, gently closing the door behind him and obtaining his surroundings. No one.

Perfect, another simple step made too easy. Now, to just keep up with him. Jason stealthily walked up the stairs and looked up at the gap in between the flights of stairs. He managed to catch his hand, gliding up the railway of the stairs and carefully following it with his precautious eyes. He still followed, going round in circles, until the hand disappeared with the sudden opening of a door being heard. Jason ran the rest of the steps and stopped where Jacob had left his hand. Looking down at the sea of pink doors. Not numbered but lettered. "Shit," he mumbled, resting his griping hand on his waist, and the other stroked his shortly cut beard that sharply defined his young face. He had no clue what to do next. He had come too far. Now what? His mind was like an Out-of-focused camera. A sudden blank blur in my mind. But it only got worse. "You don't live here. You're a stranger, aren't you?" a young voice softly said. Jason slowly drew his head up as his hidden face from his cap finally showed what was standing in front of him. A little girl with brunette hair, typically holding a ragged teddy bear. He then smiled, pulled up the legs of his trousers, crouched down onto his knees, and flicked up his cap. "Well," he sniggered, "Shouldn't you not be talking to strangers? Isn't that scary for a young girl your age?" The little girl then looked down, holding the teddy close to her small pink dress, right on her chest, and twirled slightly, pouting her lip. "Well," she spoke, now looking up with her blue eyes, "My Mommy told me that I'm the bravest girl in the world. Even if you are a stranger, mister! I am not afraid!" she finished, scrunching up her small nose. "Oh really?" he grinned. "How brave?"

"Listen, it is fine; it's no big deal," Amanda said, turning her body. "Oh really, so it's no big deal that it makes you punch your own husband. Or falsely arrest some blonde biker to be her? Not to mention, literally, make you scream in the public bathrooms!" "Yes!" Amanda said, now turning her body. "It's no big deal because I don't want you to get involved!" "Ames, no matter what, I am always going to be involved," he said, now taking her hands. "I care about you." Amanda looked down, sighed, and slipped her hands away from Jacob, stepping back from him. "Maybe this time, Jacob. I don't want you to be involved," she said, now turning her body in the other direction once more. "What's that supposed to mean!?" he called, grabbing her elbow and spinning her round again like a record player. "It means!!" she yelled, snatching her arm back. She sighed, pinched her eyes, and lowered her voice. "It means that I don't want your help." Amanda glanced her eyes up to Jacob to see him standing with his eyes pulled downwards and watched his hand continuously rub the back of his neck. "I thought this would've happened," Jacob replied more softly than ever, softer than a feather. He then dug his hand into his leather jacket pocket and pulled out a small white card. "So, if you don't want to talk to me about it," he paused, stretching his arm out to hand Amanda with the card in between his fingers, "Then it best you talk to someone else." Amanda looked at Jacob, then down at the small white card. She then slowly pinched it off Jacob's fingers and flipped it over, reading the small letters. And only rage and fear filled her body. "You're assigning me to a therapist!?" "For a good reason, Amanda!!" "No," she shook her head, "You just think I am crazy, same with Terry!" "Ames, I don't think you are crazy-" "Oh yeah!? Then why else, Jacob, why else are you giving me this!!?" she said, throwing the card to the side that flickered onto the floor. "For you to talk to someone, you're clearly being troubled with these thoughts of Bailey. Amanda, it's been five years. She has probably even forgotten about you." "Easy for you to say," She yelled, feeling her eyes fill up with warm water, making half of her vision a wet blur. "You weren't kidnapped and trapped for days! You didn't get shot by your own friend!" Amanda continued to shout, moving closer to Jacob, " You didn't starve! You didn't get your heart broken!" She cried, now near Jacob's face. "You don't know anything about what I've been through. So don't dare tell me you care like you know, as you try to address me to a therapist, like-like I'm some mental patient!" Amanda breathed, "I don't need to talk to anyone, especially not to you, Jacob!" She then, once and last time, turned herself around and walked to her bedroom, slamming the door shut. Jacob winced in anticipation and sighed. Their third fight. Their first was them being on a case, their second was in the hospital deciding about kids, and now they're third. It was about Bailey. Out of all the dramatic scenes he has encountered in their relationship. This one was by far the worst. It was like, somehow, these thoughts had created or unlocked a whole new persona for Amanda. And it wasn't pretty. Jacob softly dragged his feet over to the rectangle card lying on the floor and picked it up. He entered the kitchen and placed it onto the fridge, holding it tight by a New York magnet, and walked down to their bedroom, well more so to say Amanda's bedroom at the point. He gently knocked on the door with his stern knuckle and heard a sudden sniff. Amanda's sniff. "Amanda...I didn't mean to." He was then stopped by the door handle rattling open and the door pulling forward to Amanda standing, holding a pillow and a blanket. "Save it," she sighed, as her eyes were drowned in mascara, handing him the blankets and pillow. "It's probably the best for you to sleep on the couch tonight." "Ames, you can't be." "Jacob," she paused, "I just need the space right now." He looked into her eyes, her hurting eyes, and sighed himself. "Okay," he said, ever so soulful, and took his stuff to the couch, hearing the door close behind and flopped down. He rested one hand on his chest and the other under his head. Just looking up. "What am I going to do..."

Chapter 6: Hidden Behind The Veil

"Where are we going?" The little girl asked. She was pulled by a firm hand gripping around her small, fragile fingers, merging. "We are playing a game, a big game!" Jason said in a childish voice. He raced down the steps, each foot slapping and echoing up the building. He continued to hold the girl's hand, guiding her while she stumbled behind. "But my Mommy and Daddy will be looking for me," she almost cried, looking behind her. Jason then stopped, placed a fake stochastic smile, and placed his two manly hands on both little girls' open arms. "That's the point. We are playing hide, go seek!" He smiled. "You are brave enough to do this... right? Cause only brave girls play this game, and I'm not so sure if you're brave enough." Jason stalled and pouted childishly. "Well, I guess I'll take you back to your Mommy-" "NO!" The little girl stomped. "I'm brave! I'm brave to play!" "That's more like it." He sinisterly smiled, crouching back down on his knees. "Now...this is a big game of hide and seek. One where it can last over a night! So, we are going to work as a team to catch your Mommy and Daddy and win the game! But first, we need to plan. Okay?" "Does this mean I'm having a sleepover?" She asked innocently, rubbing her eyes. Jason sighed, rubbing his face in thought. "Yes," he said sarcastically. "It's a sleepover." The little girl blinked, looked behind her, and turned around again. "But I don't even have any pj's and plus, I don't know you, mister" "I'm Jason, an old friend of your Dad's." He lied. "And your name is?" "Stephanie," she replied, with more courage and pride.

"Stephanie?" Jason keyed, "Well, Stephanie. Now we know each other, do you trust me?" Stephanie then once again glanced behind her, holding her teddy tight. Her brown hair flicked around, and she glanced her eyes up the steps where she was far away from her apartment and cozy bed. She turned back round to look at the front door to the open street, thinking. She then looked back at Jason. She nodded but was still slightly unsure. "Good. Now, we are going to go back to my place and start a plan! Do you know what a plan is?" She quietly nodded again. "Very smart!" He laughed. "Now, you can't let Mommy or Daddy know where we are or tell anyone else cause that will ruin the game, right?" "Right". "Excellent!" Jason said, now clapping his hands. "Let the game begin..."

Jacob woke up with a sudden, painful still stiffness around his neck. He didn't have the same comfort feeling sleeping on the couch, other than their bed. His eyes felt dry and crusted like a baked desert and his brown curled hair was like staggered haystack. He groaned while lifting his body off the turn couch and flipped his legs onto the floor. The small, thin blankets fell, stroking his skin, and flopped onto the ground, still half draped over the sofa. He sighed and rubbed his hand over his face, trying to banish his tiredness, not having a clue as to what time it was. Jacob then pierced his eyes in front, his vision looking at the kitchen and saw Amanda in her sergeant uniform. Not once did she say good morning as her eyes seemed drilled onto the floor, tying her hair into a slick ponytail. But she must have seen him still on the couch asleep. Just tending to ignore him.

Amanda stroked her hair, feeling as if it was precise. She then lifted her head and met her gaze down into the living room and saw Jacob now awake and looking right at her with his pity smile. It made her feel bad, but some anger still bubbled inside her. She then turned herself round, making her way back to her room, but she stopped at her fridge as her eyes observed a small white card stuck onto a New York magnet. She snatched it off the silver door and twisted herself round to look at Jacob, still sitting down and staring, and looked at him with a stinging glare, ripping the small card in half. Amanda placed it in the bin and returned to her room. Jacob sighed, rubbing his face once more in disparity and grief, and pulled himself up onto his feet. He dragged himself down the hall and into their bedroom. "Amanda, you know I didn't mean to-" "I have to go. I'll be late for work" she replied in a provoked way. She grabbed her bag and suddenly stopped at the bedroom door. "And don't" she ceased and sighed "Don't try. I just need the space" She then walked away, without a stomp this time. But Jacob couldn't play Mr. sorrowful anymore. Instead, he also grew with anger. He did nothing wrong. He was helping her. And she was acting selfish. He then paced himself, catching up with Amanda, and slammed his hand on the door the minute she opened it to leave. "What do you think you're doing?" she sassed, looking at him with disgust and shock. "So, I'm the bad guy in this!?" "You don't understand, Jacob" she commented, opening the door again. But was slammed to a shut again by Jacob's firm hands. "Then the best I can do is to listen, but you won't even let me do that! So, what is it that you want Amanda!? I'm trying to help you!" "Help me!?" she shrieked, tied in with a sarcastic laugh "I'm sure I can help myself, after all, I did escape Bailey the first time all on my own without you! And sending me to a therapist isn't going to help me." "Oh, that's funny. Real funny. I could've sworn you wanted me to take therapy?" "That's different-" " Different? I don't see it as any different from me, your caring husband, wanting you to get help, just as you wanted me to do the same! If you won't talk to me, then who, Amanda? Who!?" Jacob looked at her, cheeks slightly a rose red from anger, and his hands still placed on the door. But Amanda didn't answer, instead, she glanced her eyes down and he slowly watched the color drain out of her. "Amanda...?" He questioned, lowering his voice, and placing his hand on her shoulder. Suddenly Amanda dropped her bag and ran down the hall, into the bathroom, and slammed the door shut. Jacob did a light jog down to the door and knocked on it. "Hey, Ames are you alright?" He then placed his ear against the door and heard coughing and gagging. Jacob then knew that she wasn't running away from him, she felt ill. He immediately felt bad, everything he said re-tracked in his head. I went too far... He still heard his wife coughing and spluttering down the toilet and decided to go into the kitchen. He rummaged through the cupboards for a glass, while his mind was spinning. He finally pulled a small glass out and filled it with water.

Jacob sped walked back to the bathroom, while small segments of water splashed onto the floor. He then suddenly heard a flush and positioned himself in front of the door. Jacob watched the handle being turned to an unlock and swung open to Amanda. Her eyes were glossy and slightly bloodshot. Her color was still slightly pale but creeping back to her natural-toned skin. Jacob held out the glass of water and smiled. Amanda looked at him, not with a smile or a glare, but just gingerly wrapped her hand around the glass and took small sips of the cold water. Silence was wrapped in the atmosphere and made it quite uncomfortable. Amanda stared at the floor and sighed. "I'm sorry..." she said, almost in a whisper. "So am I. I didn't mean to make you feel like you are crazy." He then jumped and quickened his words "Which you're not!" "Jacob. It's okay" Amanda paused "It's just..."she ceased again "I don't want you going through the same thoughts I am. It's why I didn't want to talk to you," she said now lifting her head to meet his gaze. "Amanda you've been through so much more than what I have." Jacob then placed his hands on her hips "I want to listen, and if it wasn't going to be me, then I decided that maybe someone else would be easier to talk to. But I understand that you don't agree to that-" "I Rather talk to you than anyone else. How about tonight? Me and you, just talking" she smiled. "Or maybe more..." Jacob said in a low romantic luring tone. He leaned in for a kiss, but Amanda pulled her head back. "Yeah... probably not right after I've been sick," she said with a laugh. "Oh yeah.

True, true, true. You feeling okay anyways? Hold up..." He stalled, placing his two hands on his hips "Was it me? I know I smell bad, but not-" He then sniffed his armpit "Oh god! Never mind. Me " He gagged "No, no. Adrenaline. All the shouting, stress, and anger got to me, I guess. It causes sickness and dizzy spells. Explains yesterday..." Jacob gave Amanda a sympathetic smile, he then sighed and pulled out his phone. "I'll call captain to let him know you won't be in for the bottom pr-" "No, no I'm fine! I can still go in" "You sure? You could stay home and rest. It's only one day?" "Jacob" she raised her brow and smugly smiled "Do I ever miss a day of work?" "No" He laughed, holding his phone to show the time "But it will be the second time you will be late"

"**C**rime rates are dropping low" Terry spoke, standing at the black podium. Directing his finger on an open graph chart "But that doesn't mean we do a Hitchcock and Scully, laying back and doing nothing. We still need to be up front ready like a police force" "We've had our time." Scully shouted, "We were better than you losers!" Hitchcock then commented, jabbing his finger in the air. Both best friends got up and slowly, waddled out of the briefing room. "Alright, whatever" Jacob mumbled and sighed, rising to his feet "Sarge... our beach house holiday is coming up. Couldn't we just at least chill a bit-"

"No chill, Jacob." Terry interrupted "You can "chill" when the date comes. Understand?" Jacob scoffed and looked around the room to see everyone just glaring at him. Not one person seemed to nod their head in agreement. That's until one person, who he always relied on, stepped up. "Don't worry Jacoby, I got you" Charles whispered to Jacob, standing on his two feet "Sarge. Jacob here is the most amazing detective; he is the one always on a case. Couldn't he at least get a break? Plus, if Amanda here wants a baby, I think they want alone time to be stress-free-" "Ewe, gross Charles. I'm right here." Said Amanda sitting at the desk in front, scrunching up her face in disgust. "Yeah, bit gross

Boyle" Jacob implied "But me and Amanda haven't even thought that far ahead yet. Try to Keep it in your pants" "Likewise for yourself Jacoby-" Everyone then in the room groaned, cringed and all masked their faces in disgust. "Alright. I'm out here" Terry groaned. Pulling her boots off the table and strutting her way out, slamming herself down at her desk. "Alright. Before the rest of you rudely leave. Do we understand?" Terry asked Everyone nodded in agreement, except from Amanda. Of course, she oversaw her own cases as being a sergeant. She had her own squad to deal with, but now and then she liked to still be around her own people, her own desk, and her very own captain. One by one, people exited the briefing room and went back to their attired desks. The place was always a mess. Paper, case files, crumbs, and rubbish lying all about the place. But that's what made the 99 feel like itself. It was always in a crazy manifest. Yet not as messy as Jacob's desk. Amanda was the last person to leave the room, as she gently pulled the double doors to a close. She turned herself round and saw Terry, violently clicking her mouse. Waiting for the slow Internet to connect. She then cautiously walked over to her friend's desk, like she was a ticking time bomb ready to implode. "Hey, Terry?" Amanda winced, placing her hands on her thick-waisted belt. Terry flicked her curly black hair and looked at Amanda, as per usual with no emotion. "Amanda," said Terry. Spinning round. "Listen..." she sighed "About yesterday, I'm sorry I acted all strange." "It's cool. I didn't like the place anyways." "Oh... well I-" Suddenly a voice cut off Amanda. The voice was loud and sounded unstable. A female voice. Amanda turned around to see two people stepping out of the elevator. They seemed young, around their twenties. But they weren't happy. The woman was drowned in her own tears and the man next to her, holding her by the shoulders, didn't look so happy either. "Please, s -someone help us!" The woman cried, pushing the gate and walking towards the center of the bullpen. Amanda instantly walked over to the two broken people, having her head raised higher, and greeted them with confidence.

"Hello. Sergeant Santiago of the NYPD" she said pulling at her badge pinned onto her uniform "What is it that I can assist you on?" She said calmly "M-my baby girl!" She wailed "She- she is missing. Please! You must help me to find her!" Amanda then walked over to her old desk, jumping to action immediately, and pulled out a police file document. Amanda clicked her pen vigorously and positioned her sheet properly. The couple gingerly walked over, standing, not having a clue what to do. "Take a seat ma'am" Amanda smiled. "I would like to ask a few questions. Is that okay?" "Whoever took my little girl, better be fucking sorry!" The man yelled, rubbing his face and pacing backwards and forwards. "I'm sure she is going to be okay, sir. We are going to help you" Amanda then straightened her posture and looked at the frightful Mom. "Can I have your name to start off with?" "Elisha, Elisha Fenwick. That's my husband Kai." "And your daughter's name?" Elisha paused, pursed her lips together almost ready to burst into tears again. "Stephanie. Her name is Stephanie" Kai answered. Placing two hands on his wife's shoulders. Amanda scribbled down fast on the sheet. Her head was focused, and she remained calm. It was the one thing you always had to be as a cop. Calm. "When was the last time you saw her Mrs. Fenwick?" Amanda then questioned, looking up. "We didn't mean to let her go like that! We always let her play in the hallway of the apartment building. She loves playing with her toys there. She is always such a good girl and never leaves! My baby never runs off!" "Last time seen, was the hallway of your apartment building?" "Yes!" Amanda once again buried her face into the sheet, feeling ever so sorrowful. But she then remembered those faces in front of her. Those faces were her neighbor's. "What was the last thing she was wearing?" "A pink dress. Like a classic 60's style one," she sighed but weakly smiled "Pink always brings out her eyes. Her hair was down, she was a brunette. No matter where she goes, she carries her bear. Stephanie is brave" She then looked at her husband, then back down to Amanda "But she never runs off" "She sounds beautiful, do you-" "I FOUND YOU!!" A young voice giggled. Just ahead a small girl, with brunette hair, ran across the bullpen and held out her arms, running to her Mom. Giggling. Elisha gasped in relief, cupping her hands over her mouth, and swung out her arms. She bent down on her knees and hugged her daughter. Placing her hand over her head and smiled. "Oh, my baby! You're okay! You're okay!" "I found you! I did it!" She laughed Amanda looked down at the family and smiled. It's something she has always admired. It made her heart melt. But it reminded her of Jacobs words in the briefing room. He seemed slightly off at the topic of then having a child, again. He still didn't seem to have his head wrapped around it. The husband also went down on his knees and hugged as a family. "Stephanie, baby, what happened to you?" Kai spoke, placing his hands on her face. "He helped me" she smiled, pointing behind her. Amanda looked up to see a man, standing tall and had his hands placed into his coat pockets. Smiling down at the girl. He wore a cap that slightly hid his face. But what Amanda could tell was that he was sharply defined and had a short-cut beard. His skin tone was a perfect light coffee color. Just like Amanda's slightly. Too perfect looking... "Oh sir, thank you so much," Kai said, now shaking his hand vigorously "Thank you so much" "It's no problem." He grinned, putting up his hand "This little angel just needed help to find you guys" "You're such a hero. I can't thank you enough." Elisha comments "It's no big deal, really" Amanda then stood to her feet and weakly smiled at the family. "I guess my work here is done. You guys, okay?" "Thank you, officer, thank you for the help" Kai replied. He picked up his daughter and rested him on the side of his hip. He took his wife's hands and walked back to the elevator. The little girl looked at Jason and waved her small hand goodbye. And Jason laughed, placed on a cute smile, and waved goodbye back. "Thanks for bringing her in," Amanda said in return "Oh it's not a problem, detective" "Sergeant, actually" Amanda laughed "Sergeant Santiago" Jason then started to play the acting game, playing all surprised, widening his eyes. "Amanda? As in, the Amanda Santiago?" He said, surprised Amanda laughed nervously "The one and only" Suddenly Jacob appeared back into the bullpen and looked at Amanda who was talking to a rather muscular man, slowly making his way to his desk, holding his blue-packed cup of coffee "Oh! This- this is just perfect. I was hoping to find you! I've heard so much about your work!" "My work?" Amanda questioned "About your detective work! I've heard stories about your recent escape from a blonde gal" Amanda winced at the memory. She sighed and smiled. "Sorry, I didn't catch your name?" "Jason," he said now taking off his hat, fully revealing his face. His blue eyes "Jason Anderson"

Chapter 7: In the Trance

"Jason?" Amanda said, surprised at the name "Pleasure to meet you" she said, stretching out her hand for him to shake and he gladly accepted "Thanks again for bringing her in" "Agha" He smiled, whacking his hand in the air "It's no problem. It worked better for me ending up here speaking to you" Amanda's smile creased a little more, tightening her posture in pride, and looked across her desk to see Jacob, slumped on his chair. Taking heaps of his drink and looked sourly at the man sitting next to her. Amanda decided to ignore his dull look and zipped her eyes back to Jason. "I'm flattered, really" she inhaled. "But hate to ask. why are you looking for me?" "Oh!!" He jumped, as he then twisted his body and revealed a brown shoulder bag that was dug into the chair, which Amanda never noticed at first, and unraveled it over his head. He then opened his bag and pulled out a newspaper, harshly slapping it onto her desk, and flipped out a notebook and pen. "I'm a journalist, I work for the company 'New York Times'" As he then tapped the Newspaper company title that was boldly printed across the grey, thin paper. "I was sent out to write a report on, who I think, are heroes of New York" Amanda then scoffed in surprise "And you picked me?" She questioned, unsure. "Well yeah!" He smiled "You did survive a kidnapping, beat up two guys, escaped from an Asylum, got shot, defeated Bailey while bleeding half to death, and locked up that bitch for good!" "Um" Jacob cleared his throat "I- I went through that too..." "Oh," Jason then turned "I didn't even notice you. You must be Detective Peralta?" "Indeed, I am-" "Ahh" He waved his finger "You were the one who shot Amanda" "It was an accident!" Jacob shouted, feeling his temper rise "I clearly thought she was someone else!" "Ooh" He then laughed, ignoring what he said, "You were the guy who started to fall in love with Bailey, forgetting about Amanda, got played by the villain without even knowing, and put Amanda escape right back to square one!" Jason laughed more, then sucked the air through his teeth and titled his head "That must have been embarrassing" Jacob shook with anger, having no words. He gripped his hands over the arms of his chair. Holding himself back from causing great trouble. Well... for now. "Well, actually Jacob saved me from-" Amanda's words got cut short by Jacob grabbing Jason. He wrapped his arm around his neck and violently ripped him off his chair. Jason slammed onto the floor and got turned onto his back. Everyone in the bullpen stood to their feet in shock. "Jacob!? What are you-" He immediately grabbed his shirt, pulled it up closer to him, and slammed his fist into the side of his face. "JACOB!" Amanda shouted, snapping Jacob back to reality. Realizing what he had done. He looked down at his hand which was still tightly formed into a fist, positioned like he was ready to swing another hit and back down to Jason whose hands were raised in defense. Panting. He looked around to see faces Shockley looking at him like he had three heads. Everything was sinking in slowly for him. He screwed up big time. Jacob let go, shocked by what he had done, and discreetly stood to his feet. He fixed his shirt, tugged it down vigorously, and looked at Amanda, who was shocked. Her mouth was slightly open, and her brows were knitted into a frown.

"I-I'm sorry- I just-" "What is all the commotion out here!?" A voice yelled Holt was now out of his office, standing at his door and looking directly at Jacob. "I'm sorry sir, I-" "My office, now" Jacob glanced around the room. It was so quiet. Everyone was frozen into one position. Terry stood tall on her feet; Charles sat on his desk surprised. And Amanda? She was more than shocked. Her face was riddled with emotions. It made Jacobs's heart sink down deep to his feet. Jealousy was an ugly emotion, and it got the better of him. Jacob then spun on the heels of his feet and looked down at Jason on the floor, who was now grazing his hand over the side of his face. He stretched out his arm and opened his hand for him to take. Jason looked up, then down on his open hand. He smiled weakly, slapped his hand against his, and was pulled up. "I'm sorry- I don't know what came-" "Please, please" Jason replied calmly " It's not a big deal, I was the one who took it too far..." "Peralta," Holt called Jacob paused before walking to his name. He took one last look at the man in front. So perfect. Even with the swelling bruise near his eye, he was still perfect, and those eyes. Perfectly blue. You can't blame Jacob for being Jealous. He knew that look he gave Amanda. His wife. He was flirting. It was obvious. Right? Jacob then turned, having so much shame hung to him, and walked to his captain's office, as eyes followed. It reminded him of the times in high school, being sent to the principal's office for making immature choices, like what he had just done. An immature choice. Holt gently shut the door, as Jacob sat down on one of the black-positioned seats. "Jacob." He spoke, now on his chair "Do you know why I called you in here?" Jacob looked left and right, like he thought Holt was speaking to someone else, and frowned his face. "Uh...maybe because I just beat the crap out of a journalist?" "I know you, Peralta" He sighed "You are the best detective in the 99, but not once have I ever seen you act like that. I'm flummoxed. Disappointed. So" Holt then paused, taking off his glasses and paused, Longly. "I called you in here to hear the good reason why you acted out so unprofessionally, as a detective" He looked at Holt in front with full focus and clenched his jaw. He turned round to see Amanda, through the window, continuing talking to Jason. Touching his arm. Reassuring him. He knows her pitiful smile. He then swung the background and looked down at his feet. "Jealousy." He then looked up "It's an ugly emotion"

Amanda watched the door being shut behind Jacob and sighed deeply. She looked at Jason who was grabbing his brown bag and stuffing his stuff inside. "Aw man" Terry came over, arms folded, and laughed "Never knew Jacob could swing like that!" "I'm sorry. It's my fault. I took it too far-" "You didn't" Amanda interrupted "Jacobs just..." she then looked behind, seeing him in Holt's office "He's just stressed." "I understand," He said abruptly, then making eye contact with Terry, who seemed to be analyzing him "I'm Jason" He pulled out his hand "Jason Irvin- Anderson! Anderson..."

Terry glared at him and looked at his open hand. She kept her Arms folded and looked up. "Detective Diaz" she replied. Jason looked awkwardly at her and was sharply blinking, not responding. He slowly pulled his hand away and nervously laughed. But inside, he manically laughed. They were all too easy to fool. He knew Terry's character. She was the bad bitch of the office. She sure would be fun to break... "I best be going before I cause more trouble," he said, fixing his bag. "I would like to talk more, Amanda. To get a head start on my report. Perhaps tonight?" "Tonight?" She questioned. But later that night, it was going to be her and Jacob talking. Their time. Romance time. But she wasn't happy with him. He ruined that plan. "Yeah, I'm not busy." She lied "There's a bar close by, Shaw's. Maybe there?" "Sounds great" He then handed her a piece of paper with a number on it. "Here's my number. Give me a bell when you're ready" He winked. "See you then' Amanda flushed. Flushed? She wasn't catching feelings now...was she? Jason spun his body around, ready to walk out. But briefly stopped and looked at Jacob's blue paper cup, open with coffee. Watching the steam seep out and disintegrate into the air. No lid. Perfect. Jason then looked for something to distract the girls behind. He then grabbed his head. His hat. "Oh," he said dramatically patting his head. Now turning around "You haven't happened to see my hat anywhere?" He said, swinging his head around to fakery look for it. "Um..." Amanda hummed now turning around, the same with Terry, still having her arms folded. Jason made his move. He gently pulled out an orange tube out of his coat pocket, and the tablets inside quietly shook. He popped open the white lid and gingerly shook out one small, blue tablet. It fell on the palm of his hand, and he immediately threw it into the burning coffee, making it slightly splash. "Oh!" Amanda shouted, bending over and picking up his black cap "Found it, here" She turned round to see Jason weirdly shoving his hand into his pocket quite quickly. He smiled wearily and took his cap, placing it on his dirty fur hair. "Thanks. Looking forward to tonight" Amanda watched the man strut his way back to the elevator. She noticed she was staring too much, cleared her throat, and looked at Terry, who kept her glance on him as well. "So" Terry spoke, now looking at Amanda "Jason?" "He's a journalist. He wants to write a report on me" "A report?" Questioned Terry "He thinks I'm some 'New York hero' " she quoted "And having drinks, is a good place to go?" "It's not like it's a date or anything" Amanda scoffed "It's just easier to get to, plus it's our number one place. All I'm doing is going to Shaw's, tell him whatever he wants to hear for his report, and leave it from there. You won't even hear from him again."

Chapter 8: Pink Lines

Jacob was slumped on the sofa. Flicking through the various of channels, numbing his mind. He was upset, of course. His wife was out with some journalists. God knows what they are saying, or what's going on. But his ugly emotion grew large. But he knows Amanda. He loves her, and so does she. They are married, happily married. So, nothing can get between them. Not even a journalist. Right? Sure...He may be better looking. Have a beard and even possibly abs. But that doesn't matter. No, of course not. Jacob and Amanda were a strong couple. Sure a few fights. But they were strong. But now... it felt like their relationship was weakening the minute Jason walked out them elevator doors. Jason the hero. The nerd. The 'Smart' guy. The enemy to Jacob... Jacob then leaned forward and painfully coughed. He bent his body forward and aggressively choked and spluttered. Somehow, he felt weaker. Perhaps colder too, as the hairs on his arm stood tall, trying to captivate his remaining heat. Suddenly a knock awoke at that door. Jacob cleared his throat, coughing once more, and shuffled his way to the door. He wrapped his hand around the handle and swung it open, waiting it to be Amanda still in her mood. In fact, it was just Terry. She looked at Jacob and her eyes narrowed in contempt. "Dude. You don't look so good" she said, looking at him up and down. "Yeah" He rasped "I'm starting to catch something." He then opened the door fully and stepped to the side "Come on in" Terry walked in discreetly, looking around the room. "Is Amanda home?" She asked, now setting down a plastic bag onto the dinner table, that Jacob never noticed or felt bothered to ask. "No, she still out with Jason" He said his name in disgust. Then coughing once again "Is Ashley with you?" "Nope. She is at home. Packing" "I suppose as it's only a day away till we go..." Jacob thought. Realizing he wasn't prepared for the beach house at all "What made you call over so late?" "Auh..." she stalled, glancing her eyes at the plastic bag. "Just wanted to check up on you guys. To see if you are okay" "Well. We are still fighting. That's for sure" He sighed. Sitting back down and wrapped himself in a blanket. "I know Amanda," she said, now sitting next to him "We both know her. I'm sure she is going to step through that door, saying it was a boring time and he is finally gone back to his nerd lab" "AGH!" A voice yelled, and a sudden slam. Amanda stumbled into the apartment, wobbling. "THAT WAS TOTALLY A GOOD TIME!!!" she said, pointing both fingers high to the sky. Terry then nervously smiled at Jacob who was groaning in disparity at his own wife. "See?" She laughed "Such a boring time..."

Minutes passed after Jason dropped off a very drunk Amanda. What an idiot she is. She doesn't even know how much she is destroying her love life with sad old Jacob. But he endured the thought. Oh, how things were going to plan. He didn't need the help, he realized. He can work alone. Bailey was no match for him. He has been in worse situations. He was doing better than her. What's she doing? All locked up in her cell. Useless. Jason gripped his wheel. The night was dark, and the orange lights glowed in the streets. He came to a red light and his car slightly jolted forward to the break. He looked at his right hand. His ring reflected in the orange light. He lost his thoughts just looking at it. The world around him began to sink away.

That ring meant so much to him, at one point. Now it was just a piece of gold around his finger. Having no reason behind it. Only having memories, sadness, and aggression. Tears filled his eyes. For a strong man, this was the one thing that broke him. The one thing that made him cry. How dare she? How could she? She? Who is she? "I'm so sorry April..." He choked. "You just couldn't give me what I wanted." His mind snapped back as a loud horn honked behind him. The light was green. He flipped off to the guy behind and stepped his foot on the pedal. Jolting and zooming down the street. His new apartment wasn't far, only blocks away from the Police department. It wasn't the best place, just a little something for now during his planning. It was old, but nothing too bad. Nothing like the type of old grubby apartments you see on TV. Just the typical muffled fight you can hear, banging, or the unexpected faint squeak of a bedrock. His wheels began to slow and bump up a kern, Stopping his car in a park. He then swung his door open and stepped outside. His car keys clattered as he Walked into the building, smuggled with the toxic smell of cigarettes. Jason skipped up the steps, two steps at a time, and reached the third floor. He looked down the, not too bad hallway, and softly walked over to his door. Number 24. His key slid in smoothly, and it clicked to an unlock. His door creaked open, and he stepped inside and flicked the lights on. "Aww...." a voice slithered "Was poor baby Jason crying?" Just in front of him, Bailey was draped over an old single chair. Her legs rested on one of the Arms of the couch as her feet were crossed nicely. Her face was an evil smug as she rested her two hands over the back of her head. "What are you doing here!?" Jason spoke through his gritted teeth and closed his door "Aren't you supposed to be in jail still!?" "Got out early," she said smiling. Now strangely having a knife in her hand, cleaning the dirt out of her fingernails. "How?" She then laughed shortly through her nose. "Ask no questions. Get no lies" "Whatever. And I wasn't crying" He added. Setting his keys down on the unit next to him. "Sure, you weren't big boy," said Bailey. Now sitting properly on the set having her legs crossed. "So, where were you this late? Anything interesting that I need to hear?" "I was out with that Santiago girl." "Ahh yes. The freak. What are the details? Fill me in," Jason sighed, hating the fact that he had to team up with his own sister. Couldn't he just do everything himself? He was enjoying it. "Her and Jacob are married. I saw the ring on her finger, the same with that man. They live in her apartment together. Not far from here" "Aww...How cute, married already." She said sarcastically "Anything else on the detectives?" "Amanda isn't a detective" He paused "She is a sergeant" "Well, well, well. Look at her grow! Eh? Little Amanda seems to be climbing the top." She sinisterly laughed. "She was always a competitive rat. Wanting to be the best." Bailey then stood to her feet "What were you doing with her tonight?"

"Collecting details, well supposed to as she got a bit hammered, but like you asked. I'm acting all Mr. journalist, as you apparently just sit here and do nothing. While I, on the other hand, have been doing a little more than just grabbing details." He said, now lifting out the small orange tube of pills. He then chucked them to his sister, and she caught them perfectly.

"You know," she said, shaking the bottle "I had my doubts about you. Thinking you were still weak over April. Depressed. But you have really come out of your shell." "April is none of your business," Jason said bitterly. "I'm just saying," she shrugged "It's time to let go." She then walked over to him, looking up slightly as he was taller, and took his hand "Maybe by getting rid of this" She then started to pull off his ring. But Jason snatched his hand back and glared at her firmly. "I said it was none of your business." Bailey raised her two hands in surrender and stepped back. "Alright...Alright...oh!" She then sniggered "I almost forgot. I brought company!" "Company? What is this, some party?" "Come on out" "JACOB!" Amanda shouted, snapping Jacob back to reality. Just then, a tall man with brown, curly hair stepped out from the corner of the apartment building. He had broad shoulders and toned arms. His skin was swarthy and clear, his eyes were green, and his face was toned. He wore a black shirt and tight skinny jeans. "Shea...meet Jason, my brother" she smiled "Jason, Shea. An old friend" "I'm not here to make friends." Jason replied. "Who said we are friends?" Shea scoffed "I only smiled because Bailey said to smile, and to also make a good impression because you're "complicated" and she wasn't lying." Jason rolled his eyes send folded his arms. "I see you are quite the asshole" He added "What's your reason for being here? Obviously, you have a hate against someone" "I'm here to take the 99 on their knees, especially Amanda. I hate that little bitch." He growled, inhaling "In high school me and Ashley were so close to being best friends and then Amanda, smart little Amanda, came along and basically stole Ashley. Started being friends and left me out. I had no one." He paused "No one." "Waw did not expect a whole back story. Sounds like you and Bailey have a lot in common." Jason replied dryly. "Indeed, we do brother. Shea here also got arrested by the slut. He-" "Bailey" Shea interrupted "Don't step on my moment. Anyways, I robbed Ashley. Out of hate. But Detective Amanda saved the day. Caught me. Threw me behind bars for 4 years." "What?" Jason said, confused "Just for stealing stuff? That can't be 4 years" "I tried to kill the Nerd." He said deeply. "After she found me, I tried to attack the whore." "Great. Amanda started a cult." He joked. Bailey then clapped her hands in glee. Laughing. "God. That story puts a smile on my face." She clapped "So, where are the two love birds now?" "Back their apartment. Like I said. Plus, I'm sure these little blue babies are working right now." Jason said. Pointing at the orange tub "Tomorrow, they have no chance" Bailey rolled her eyes and raised to her feet. Jason watched her step over to his kitchen and grabbed a beer. She whacked it against the edge of his counter, busting open the cap. She bent her head back, taking heaps of the alcohol. She then slammed the bottle down. "We need a plan" She gasped. Wiping her mouth. "I'd say you give me some of that beer then I'll start talking," said Shea, putting out his hands, waiting.

Bailey lifted a cold one out of the fridge and chucked it over to Shea. He caught it, and also slammed it against the closest unit for the cap to bust open. "Can you please stop slamming beer caps on my shit?" Jason yelled, getting more annoyed. Shea then scoffed. Setting his drink down. "Once you come up with a smart idea that we can Go with, maybe I suppose we can" "Can you two dickheads stop the moaning?" She provoked. "Oh. Of course," Shea paused "That's Amanda's job... whiny bitch" "Back to the plan, idiot" Bailey stressed, now back in the center of the living room. "This time. We need to lure only the two of them. Somewhere slightly far from the city" "You mean making the same plan. Like last time?" Jason asked "The whole school incident? Waw. Real ogrishly" "Well, Fuck face. It worked, didn't it?" "What about the others?" Shea asked. The room filled with quietness.

Thoughts were passing about. "I wouldn't worry about them just yet" Jason finally spoke "They have a vacation coming up, in a beach house. Up north." "Yes..." Bailey mumbled, smiling "It will give us enough time to sort out Jacoby and little Santiago. Then, we bring them in" She then snapped her fingers "The asylum! It's a perfect place" "Of course it is..." "Yeah, but how do we lure them there without making it noticeable?" Shea said. Jason then flopped down onto his couch but felt something soft poking his back. He wrapped his arm behind him and pulled out what was behind. In his hands, he held a teddy. The little girl's teddy. "I think I have an idea..."

"**A**manda, you need to sit down," Jacob said, annoyed at her. "Okays" Amanda then flopped on the floor, Giggling. She then looked up at Terry "Wow. You look so tall" "Alright, get up," said Terry, grabbing Amanda by under her arms. But Amanda didn't put any effort to stand on her feet. She let her body go loose, leaving Terry to struggle to lift her. "Amanda!!" She gasped "At least give me some help!!!" "This is fuuuuun" Terry then let go, letting her flop back down onto the floor as she drunkenly yelled in pain. Terry rolled her eyes and once again lifted her. Finally, Amanda decided to act on her demand and stood to her feet. Wobbling. "I'll go get her pajamas" Jacob replied, still very annoyed. "Amanda. Can you come to the bathroom for a second?" Terry asked. "I'll only hold your hand. But I'm not wiping you-" "Stop! That's not what I'm asking!" She yelled in disgust. She then picked up a plastic bag "I need you to do something" "Oh, okay" she laughed "But nothing too dirty. I have a husband-" "Dear god, just come" Terry then grabbed Amanda by her wrist and dragged her behind. They both entered the bathroom, as she locked the door behind. Terry then set down the plastic bag and turned to her friend. "I know you are drunk. But you must do this now," She then reached into the bag and lifted out a pregnancy test. "Omg, Terrasa, you're pregnant!?" "What? No. You might be. All this sickness and mood swings are signs, and I checked your calendar. You're 3 weeks late" "You got into my computer and looked at my calendar? How did you even know I kept my information there?" She slurred, confused. "It doesn't matter" She then ripped open the box "All you have to do, is pee. Got it?" "I have loads of pee" "Gross" she replied "Listen. Do this and find out the results. Two pink lines are positive. One line is negative. Text me immediately. I must go" Terry swung open the door, closing it behind her. She then saw Jacob in the other room getting Amanda's bed ready. His face seemed annoyed, hurt, and stressed. Having a drunk Amanda was not easy, or fun. It hurt him more that obviously, she had a good time with Jason. God knows what happened. He continued to sniffle and cough vigorously and violently. Folding her pajamas on the end of the bed. "Hey" Terry knocked at that door to catch his attention "I'm going here. I'll see you tomorrow?" Jacob coughed once more and cleared his throat. Standing tall on his feet. "Sure," he said softly. "Hey, before you go. What were you saying to Amanda in the bathroom?" Terry didn't want to tell him. It wasn't her job, and it might be a negative comeback. A false alarm. So, she avoided it. "Uh... nothing important. Just, girl stuff." Jacob didn't seem too convinced, but he nodded his head anyways. "Alright. I'll see you tomorrow then" "Cool, later" Terry left their apartment, as Jacob heard the door being closed. He sighed and rubbed his face. Trying to push his tiredness away. Jacob shuffled out of the bedroom and stopped at the bathroom door, just looking at it. He said nothing and carried on walking back to his sofa, collapsing down on it. At the same time, Amanda was in the bathroom. Waiting on the results. The white stick sat on the bathroom unit. It probably wasn't even the best time. Amanda was still awfully drunk. Her vision was like an out-of-focus camera and her mind was a jumbled mess. She sat on the side of her bath, waiting. Minutes passed, so surely it was ready now. Amanda went over and picked up the stick. One line. "Putt...pregnant" she scoffed, throwing it in the bin next to her and opening the door. She saw Jacob passed out on the sofa down the hall, having two bits of tissue stuck up his nose. Amanda dragged herself down the hall and into the living room and curled up next to her husband, immediately drifting off. Knowing well she wasn't pregnant. Well, that's what she thought. Inside her bathroom bin sat a pregnancy test. A pregnancy test with two pink lines.

Chapter 9: Dilemma

Jacob's eyes fluttered open. Amanda's alarm was ringing in his ears. It sounded too close as it was excruciating. He then pulled his eyes down to see his wife curled up next to him on the sofa, passed out still. Not even she woke up to her alarm. He discreetly reached over and grabbed her phone that was next to her and switched off the taunting ring. He looked back down to Amanda, whose hair was a mess and plastered to her face. Drool dribbled out of the side of her mouth and her eyes were caked in mascara. To him, it was cute. He tried so hard not to wake her, as he wanted to make her something special. He knew fine rightly that she was going to wake up with a banging hangover and knowing her, she would push through it and still go to work. It's Amanda. He then lifted her head off his shoulder and tried to gently place it on the cushion of the sofa. But she groaned and opened her eyes. Squinting "Urh... God." Amanda moaned. Covering her eyes. "Morning" Jacob replied. Not sounding too sweet about it "My head feels like it's getting hit with a sledgehammer" she rasped. Covering her head and sitting up. "I'll get something to help" Jacob then rushed to the kitchen and started rummaging through the cupboard. Amanda, in the living room, rubbed her eyes and pulled her hair out of her face, and suddenly coughed a little. She then got her eyes adjusted and yawned. She just took a minute and sat there, soaking up the pain and looking around her apartment. Her eyes were then drawn to her bag by the door that had everything spilled out. Lipstick, purse, pens, glasses, a torch, and an orange tube that mostly caught her attention. She decided to pull to her feet, wobbling to her fuzzy sight, and walked over to the orange object that was shaking her curiosity. She has never seen it before. She went down to her knees and picked it up and a couple of pills inside rattled. There was a label stuck to it. But not a label saying what exactly it was. It was a handwritten label. 'For your hangover :)

Jason' Amanda slightly laughed and popped open the cap. She tipped out a fresh pill that was so boldly blue and observed it. The small circular pill was so tiny, but Amanda didn't know what drug it was. Painkillers maybe? Of course, it was. Jason must have it to her last night. He knew she was a mess. So, why wouldn't they be painkillers? Jason is no criminal. "Hey," Amanda called, now going to the kitchen. "You are okay, I have some painkillers here," she said, showing the orange tube. Jacob then horrifyingly coughed. "Where-" He coughed again "Where did you get them?" "Jason must have placed them in my bag" "Oh. Of course. Jason" Jacob said sarcastically "The journalist" Amanda then sighed and slammed the orange tube onto the counter. "You know. I thought we would be over this?" "Over what?" "Oh, come on, Jacob. Don't play dumb with me. Over Jason, I know you are jealous of him" "Jealous!?" He scoffed, placing his hands on his hips "Not jealous. Just concerned. You did come home extremely drunk last night. God knows what happened" "You saying you don't trust me?" Amanda asked bitterly "No, did you hear me say those words?" "You know what Jacob?" she then placed the pill into her mouth and swung back the glass of water Jacob previously poured for her "I'm done talking to you. Until you finally grow up and have trust in me. Then we can talk"

"Fine!" he replied "Fine!" Amanda went to her room to get ready. All the yelling made her feel worse. She suddenly felt a whole crash of weakness and a feeling of illness. She then bent over and coughed, like she couldn't stop. It was Scratching her vocals and tightening her lungs. Maybe she was catching what Jacob seemed to have. Jacob, in the kitchen, sniffled and tried to shake his dizziness away. Minute by minute, he seemed to be getting worse. His coughs became more violent, and his temperature was rising like a hot air balloon. He looked at the pills, lying in the tub and considered taking one, maybe to ease off his sore throat. He then lifted it, tipping one into his hand. Jacob stalled, glaring at it. He tipped another one and threw both into his mouth. In the other room, Amanda coughed and coughed. But not as bad as what Jacobs was. She made her way to the bathroom, now shivering. She closed the door behind her and suddenly felt a sneeze coming. She ripped a piece of toilet paper and sneezed into it. Feeling mucus pile onto it. She was sick. For sure. Caught it off Jacob perhaps. She sighed and decided to throw it into the bin. That's until she froze. Her eyes met upon something that brought back a memory from last night. Inside the bin, sat her pregnancy test. It wasn't negative. It was positive. Two little pink lines. Pregnant. She couldn't believe it; how could she forget? She is pregnant and Jacob doesn't know. This is it. She was going to become a Mom. That's all she wanted in life. But now she was scared. Amanda wasn't ready. It wasn't the perfect timing. Would Jacob leave her after this? She had to hide it for now. She couldn't possibly let him know. Not when they are fighting. The only person she could tell was Terry. She would know what to do. But all that was on her mind, is that her child was growing within her, right at this minute. It was a miracle. But a bad-timing miracle. Amanda then picked up the stick from the bin and placed it in her sink cupboard that was filled with lady materials. Jacob never looks in here. So, it's a perfect place. She slammed it shut, sighed like the heavyweight was off her shoulders, and stood there. She then looked at her own reflection. She looked awful. Amanda looked sick. Her nose seemed slightly red, and her eyes looked dull. Her natural color was gone. She felt like hell. And just at that moment, she bent over and coughed again. This time it was a little bit more aggressive than the last. Amanda opened the door and quickly glanced at Jacob who was still in the living room. Even he didn't look too good. He looked worse than Amanda. He was practically grey; his eyes were bloodshot, and he seemed to be shivering. But. None of this was going to stop Amanda from going to work. So, she decided to get ready.

"**A**nd where were you!?" Bailey shut the front door and stopped at her living room opening to her Dad's voice, having her school bag still strapped to her back, and kept her eyes attained onto the wooden floor and sighed. "I got held behind in school," she said with no emotion, knowing this was going to escalate. "And why were you held behind?" He said so grimly and luring. Standing to his feet.

"Does Mommy still love me?" "Of course," He paused "Perhaps not your sister at the minute. But you, my boy" he laughed, now placing him on his lap. "Will make her and me proud" Bailey gave up the screaming and slid down to the floor. She crossed her arms over her legs and buried her face, crying. Her home wasn't a mess. It was very modern-looking. She had good clothes, a clean room, and reasonable food. Yet inside. She was living in IA n hostile. A family with a lost Mom who created a banished abusive father. They hated his daughter. The daughter that reminded him of his loved one. The next day arrived for Bailey. Another day in school, her escape. Luckily, she was popular. Everyone knew her. The pretty blonde, yet with the weird childish boyfriend. Jacob. She couldn't wait to see him. She loved him. He was hers. No one else. She saw the door opening to her Dad, he didn't say a word. But walked away. She raced up to her room and put on her best clothes that brought out her figure. She was ready to see Jacob. He cares about her. He loves her. No sooner or later Bailey raced outside and made her way to school. She was greeted with many waves and girls whispering in jealousy. Boys' eyes followed her as she walked with pride. Just inside the school, Jacob stood by her red locker, hands in his pockets, waiting for her. She skipped over to him and kissed him on the cheek, causing him to snap out of his daze as he had been staring at the floor. "Hey Jacoby!" she giggled "Well... How do I look? " Bailey posed, showing off her outfit. A tight red checkered skirt with a white turtleneck shirt. Her hair was curled, like always. "Um...yeah. You look great" he said recklessly "Hey?" she said, placing her hand on his Arm "What's wrong?" "Tay" Jacob inhaled. "We need to talk" She knew those words. "Sure... What's up?" she said timidly, folding her arms. "I don't know how to say this but" He Paul, Ed "You're great and all, but." He ceased again. Looking at her "Bailey, I love someone else" Her heart crushed. "What do you mean, you love someone else!? Who!!?" "Her name is Eliza..." "The Nerd!!!?" "She is kind and smart. I'm sorry... But this isn't working out for us." "But I thought you loved me!? We are supposed to be the best couple in the school!?" "That's all you care about, the popularity. I don't really fit into that. Eliza... Is more of my type" "Your type is nerds?" "She isn't a Nerd Bailey!!" She then scoffed "Push, yeah. Right, okay" "I'm sorry. But you must let go" "Jacoby..." Jacob walked away, back to his new girlfriend. She was a brunette, glasses and holding books. Nerd material. Oh, how Bailey hated nerds. How she hated Eliza. How she hated all little, smart freaks who got in her way. Bailey looked at her locker. There, she had their initials carved into the metal door. J & T. revealing the true grey color behind the red paint and, she cried.

"I haven't lost you yet..." "Bailey?" a voice echoed, and her vision went black. She awoke, sweating. It was all a memory, all a dream. In front stood Jason, looking down at his sister who was sleeping on his couch. "What do you want?" She snapped "You were dreaming. You kept mumbling Dad's name and mine. Even Jacobs. What the hell were you dreaming?" "It's none of your business, that's what," she said, now sitting up. "What? Were you watching me or something?" "Uh, no. I need to talk to you" "And it better be good" "The plan?" He dragged "Hello? That's the reason why I'm here So get up and get your little friend Shea to wake his ass. I've brought a little friend" "Friend?" Bailey questioned. "Well..." he sniggered. "Maybe more than just 'A friend'" he quoted, then kicking Shea in the back who was sleeping on the floor. "Oi, rat. Get up" "Gah" He groaned, rubbing his back "You know? You can do other things to wake a person up like, shake them! Not kick them you psychotic bitch!" Shea then got up and slammed him to the wall, ready to punch him. "Boys!" Bailey yelled "Fuck's sake. Do I really need to get you two, a get-along shirt!? God almighty..." Shea glared at Jason, and he glared back. He let go, fixing the same clothes as yesterday, and stepped back. "Why are you waking us at this time?" Shea said checking his phone "At Eight in the morning?" "I'm sorry... Did I ruin your little sleepover party?" Jason mocked, putting a childish voice on. Shea sighed and flopped on the sofa, putting his arm on top. "Just answer the question and stop getting on like everything is a competition" "I brought some company." He then went to a small door, that was a cupboard for coats and shoes. Inside lay a little girl unconscious and Sophia. Both have gags around their mouths. "Okay. Who are they? And why are they in your coat cupboard?" Said Shea, sitting uprightly now. "Is this a part of the plan?" Bailey questioned. "The little girl, yes. The brunette? No, she isn't. Is that okay with you, Tay? Or would you like to stick to the schedule like a little Amanda Santiago?" "You fucking dare call me that" she threatened. But Jason just laughed. "I was thinking last night. Thinking a lot. Bailey, you want to be close to Jacob, closer than ever? Right?" "Yes, get to the point" "Then we need her. She can help us" "With what?" Bailey asked. Looking at the two hostages. "What the hell!? You think kidnapping is going to get us any further than we are? I said innocence shouldn't be caught up in this. The nine-nine are the only ones we can hurt. I'm so sorry you look like Jessica and Delphine, so I'm going to call them that. I don't want to know their real names" Shea said. Jason rolled his eyes in disparity. "Gosh. Didn't know you were a big softie. Do you want revenge on Amanda or not?"

"Look, I may be spiteful, but I'm not placing innocent people on this" Shea. "You have joined us, now is not the time to turn your back on us." Bailey glared. "I may hate Amanda. But I'm not dragging a little girl into this" "Don't worry, they won't get hurt." Jason smiled. "I still don't understand. How is the brunette going to help me get closer to Jacob?" Bailey asked. "This is how..." Jason then handed over paper that was discreetly folded up. It was creased and crushed. But Bailey pinched it off his hand. She opened it up and traced her eyes over the letter. "Brother." she looked up, smiling. "Best be making invitations soon" she laughed.

Both Jacob and Amanda stubble into the precinct. Coughing and looking ill. To Amanda's surprise. Jacob was pushing to go to work, something that usually doesn't happen. Amanda felt awful, the painkillers weren't working. The same for Jacob. He just felt worse. Plus, that wasn't the only thing that was on her mind. She was pregnant. What about the amount of alcohol she had last night? Does that have an effect? "OH, dear god. You two look like zombies" Ashley said in disgust, seeing them walk out of the elevator. "Thanks, Ashley," Jacob said dryly, going to his desk and weakly sitting down. Ashley then walked over to Amanda and smugly smiled. "So little Zombie... What's the news?" Ashley giggled. "What are-" Amanda coughed. "What are you talking about?" "You know." she leaned in closer. "The P, R, E, G, -" "You know about that!?" Amanda shouted in a whisper. Glancing her eyes about. "Terry tells me everything." "Of course..." Suddenly, Amanda heard a shallow clack of heels. Terrys heels. "You didn't text me," Terry said, almost annoyed. "Sorry that I passed out, Terry!" she replied sarcastically. "Bathroom, we will talk there" All three walked into the ladies' room and stood in a circle. Well, Terry and Ashley are side by side, looking at Amanda. "Yes," Amanda sighed. "Yes? Yes, what?" Terry said impatiently. "I'm p.re-" Amanda bent over and sneezed more than once and finished it off with a cough. "Sorry. Pregnant. I am pregnant." "Ugh... And real sick. You going to make it to the beach house like this?" said Ashley, standing back. "Yeah. I'll just try to take it easy today." "About the pregnancy. Does Jacob know?" Terry asked. "We aren't on speaking terms. So, no. He doesn't and I want this kept for now. Understand?"

"Yes, and you keep 2 meters away from me. Maybe isolation?" said Ashley "Ashley, it's not a virus. I just have the cold." "Yeah? Well, you sound like Kermit the frog" "I agree" Spoke Terry "You really don't look good and Jacob." "I'll be fine. It's not going to kill me."

Seconds, minutes, and hours went by, and Jacob was still slumped in his chair. He has done nothing but just sit in his chair. Sneezing. Coughing and filling cases. Collecting perp names and almost sleeping. He drank so many coffees that it started to make him shake. It slightly helped. But his head felt heavy, mouth was dry, and his nose blocked. He hasn't seen Amanda since she walked out of the bathroom with Ashley and Terry. It was 9pm and people were almost ready to leave for the beach house. Jacob packed, even Amanda's bag when she was with Jason. So, they were ready. "So, Ashley. You packed?" Jacob managed to speak. "Hell yeah, four bags packed" she laughed Suddenly, Amanda walked across the bullpen, holding a box and taking it to her desk. Not looking at Jacob. She seemed exhausted, tired, and sick. Jacob heard her coughing. Maybe she caught what he had. "So, Amanda," Ashley called "I guess this is the time to see Seven Drink Amanda? Or even ten! We all know Nine Drink speaks French." Suddenly Amanda stuttered. Ed "Uh... I don't feel like drinking Ashley. You know? Just not this holiday. It's time for a break," she said, trying to remind her of the real reason to no drinking while pregnant. "Oh...YES! Yes. Of course. Well, that doesn't stop Terry from drinking." she then went over and placed her arm around. Terry "It brings out her soft side." "It does not. Anyways. I'll see you guys tomorrow?" "Sure," Jacob said, and Amanda nodded. "Beach House here we coulee!" Ashley cheered, leaving the precinct. Charles then came over with a large smile on his face "So, this is the perfect opportunity for you two to make three! All thanks to my beach house. We have many rooms" He then leaned in closer "And even a special room" Both Amanda and Jacob groaned in disgust. "Boyle. For once, let it go" said Jacob, cleaning his nose "Like I said, we haven't got that far. We aren't ready. Plus... Some of us need to worry about other things" He then glanced at Amanda who was looking at him spitefully. "Well. It's never too late! I'll catch you guys tomorrow. It's going to be a par-they" And just like that Boyle left and so did Terry. Jacob and Amanda were left. Ready to leave, that's until they got pulled by Captain Holt. "Peralta, Santiago. I got a phone call" "What is it, sir?" Amanda said in contempt. "The little girl that was here yesterday. Has gone missing again. The kidnapper left a message on where she is. The mother of the child was on the phone there. She couldn't describe the person as she randomly blacked out. We need to find her" He sighed "I would gather the others, but they are already home" "Where? Where is she?" Jacob asked. Now have a heap of energy. Holt paused and looked at Amanda. "The Asylum." Those words made Amanda shutter. It slid down her spine and filled her veins with fear. She can't go back to the memories. She couldn't. "No- I can't. I'm not going back there" Amanda shook her head "I can't" "You're the only two here. She needs our help" Holt demanded. Amanda looked at Jacob, forgetting their fight, and sighed. A little girl was in danger. Imagine if that was her kid? What would she do? "We find the girl, bring her back safely" Amanda sighed, looking at Jacob. "Then, we head to the beach house the next day" "We will catch the guy and find her. You have our word sir" "Make sure you are in contact, in case for back up. I'll be by my radio. You guys will be fine" Amanda dropped her stuff and followed Jacob down into the locker room. It was all like the past. Getting ready for the active shooter. Amanda had to swallow her fear and push past the thoughts. Sure, what could go wrong?

Chapter 10: Sinking In

Outside, the sky was a dark sheet of pure blackness. Stars glowed vividly and building lights glowed in the distance. The air was crisp and damp as rain bounced off many cars. Jacob and Amanda drove farther away from the city. Across the Brooklyn Bridge to cross the other burrow to reach their checkpoint. The car journey wasn't long. But it sure was quiet. But thankfully, the muffled pitter-patter of the rain swarmed and swallowed the sound of nothing between them. Amanda sat on the passenger side of the car. Her mind was too preoccupied with thoughts. She couldn't possibly have the focus to be behind the wheel. So many clogs were turning in her head. What was she doing? Going back to a place that caused her so much damage and hurting memories? But on the other side of her mind. She was saving a little girl. A poor mother was crying for her little girl. Amanda had to step up, be the real cop, and ignore her worries. Or at least try to. Her head was still slightly sore but fading off. But her sickness remained. She was sweating but not out of fear. Her chest felt tighter, and her persistent cough still clung to her like glue and Jacob wasn't looking any better. For him, he was cold. Shivering. His coughs scratched his throat like sharp small blades and his energy dropped levels deep. His eyes felt like heaps of concrete and his nose was blocked. His face was so pale almost like he was dead. That type of pale. Except, under his eyes, yellowish or-angery rings sat underneath. Around his nose was the same. It was almost like he had an apocalyptic virus. He couldn't take it anymore. He needed something to ease it off. "Amanda. Tell me you brought the" he coughed "Those painkillers" he rasped. "Uhm, should do," she said, checking her pockets to then wrap her fingers around an object "Got it. Here" Amanda handed over the tube. Jacob took one hand off the wheel and flicked open the white cap with his thumb. He then didn't hesitate to throw in three more little pills inside his mouth and swallow. "Getting worse?" Amanda asked softly. "Yeah. I don't know what the hell it is. But it's killing me" he said sternly. Still has his eyes on the road. Amanda then took back the pills and placed two in her hand. "I caught what you have," she said, now throwing back the pills into her mouth "Hopefully these will help for the time being." She then placed them back into her pocket and looked up. Ahead, just over a hill. Stood the very building itself. So, abandoned. No other buildings surrounded it. Only heaps of dead grass and trees. It was far away from the city. Jacob then passed the rusted gates and drove very observantly to the building. Green painted the bricked outside walls. Windows were bombarded with wooden planks and darkness filled the building. It was just like Amanda remembered. The car came to a soft brake and their eyes both glanced up. Just looking at it. Amanda pulled her gaze away and looked down at her feet. Her heart was pounding. Her mind was swimming in the thoughts. She couldn't back out now. Here they were. "Jacob" she spoke, still looking down "I'm sorry for everything" Jacob looked at his wife, who still didn't look up, and sighed sadly. She was clearly scared and didn't want to lose him. "Ames, it's alright," he took her hand "No matter what. I will always love you. I just care." Amanda then looked up with a frown on her face and looked at Jacob. Smiling in pity.

"I'm scared." "I know you are. But that little girl in there needs us. Needs you. Amanda" he paused "You're the strongest woman I have ever met. You have overcome so much. So don't let this back you down. You got this, and I am by your side. So" Jacob inhaled "Bring your tall, weird butt out here, save the little girl, and before you know it. It's vacation time!" Amanda laughed. Something that felt good and kissed Jacob. Cupping her one hand on his face. "I love you" she whispered. "Love you too" Jacob replied. They then broke their moment and jumped out of the car. Jacob took out his flashlight and glazed it on the building. He then brought it down to the double doors, that were oddly open. He then held the button of his radio, sitting on his bulletproof vest. "This is Detective Peralta and Sergeant Santiago. We reached the permitted location and are heading in. Do you copy? Over" He released the button. No response. Just a static noise. He looked at Amanda in curiosity. She only shrugged and started to cough again.

He held it in once again "Does anybody copy? Over" Nothing. "Stupid Radio signal!" Jacob groaned "Let's just go." They both stealthily walked in. Guns aiming high, as in the other hand crossed beneath, held a torch. The hallways were dark and musty. Grey paint was peeling off walls, curling and rotting away. The tiles were covered in greenery and mud and the smell was intoxicating. Jacob then suddenly bent over and coughed. Not once, but multiple. It hurt like hell. It felt like blazing lava erupting up his esophagus. His sight was unstable, and his eyes felt like they were ready to depart from his face. "Jesus, Jacob. You okay!?" Amanda said. I'm so worried now. He coughed one more time. "Fine." coughed again "Fine. Just, keep going. It's alright." Amanda frowned but nodded and walked ahead. Jacob then stood tall and looked down at his hand. He shakily inhaled and wiped away the stuff on his hand. His blood. He then followed behind Amanda, watching her every move, and also looked about. He remembered some of it. The same for Amanda. It sent chills down her. Amanda then sneezed "Aww... That was cute" She rolled her eyes and sniffed. Suddenly, a sudden sound shambled down the hall, like something metallic dropped. They both spun around, pointing their guns in the other direction. "You heard that. Right? It's not just my sicknesses playing more games?" Jacob said, looking around. "Yeah... I did." It was then the echo stopped and they were standing together, pulling their flashlights in every little corner they could find. Just glancing their eyes about in precaution. "Rats. Might be just rats" Jacob said. Trying to reassure himself. "Oh, yeah. Rats playing a little band with whatever metallic object. Good one Jacob" "Let's keep looking. I'm sure-" Suddenly a swooping sound whizzed past Amanda's ear. She heard Jacob groan, grabbing the back of his neck. Amanda flashed her flashlight on him and saw Jacob holding up a small little dart.

Just like that. His eyes rolled to the back of his head and shattered to the floor. "JACOB!?" "Aww. What a shame." Amanda spun round and pointed her flashlight down the hall, and never has she felt more afraid in her life. "T-Bailey" she shook. "Aww, look. She remembers me!" she said, nudging Shea on the shoulder next to Bailey. "Although, my name doesn't have two T's" she laughed. "How could I not forget about you? You caused me pain, Irvine." Amanda replied sternly, then looked at Shea "Who's this?" Shea then scoffed, then let out a laugh. "Honestly, quite rude to forget one of the best criminals to walk the earth. Of course, we didn't get much time to chat. You did stick hand-cuffs on me and threw me in jail before I could defend myself. But trust me" He then flipped out a shank "You won't forget me this time" He then charged at her, and Amanda pointed the gun and shot. But she was just in time, he pulled the muzzle down and the gold-flamed bul-let ricocheted off the floor in a ping. Amanda pulled her eyes up to Shea, and he grinned in glee. He then twisted her arm. Making her gasp in pain and drop her weapon as it slapped to the floor. She felt weak. Weaker now without a weapon. But the sickness was overwhelming her defenses. Tackling her down. Shea then punched her in the stom-ach, winding Amanda and making her lean over and struggle for air. Shea grabbed her by the throat and slammed her to the rotting wall, pulling all his force. Amanda scratched at his hands and had the need to cough "You're lucky she is watching" Shea threatened, nodding his head at Bailey who was standing watching with a smile, of crystalline joy. Arms folded. He then leaned in closer to her face. "Or you would've already been 5 meters deep underground. Now, night" Shea then smug-gled Amanda's mouth with a cloth. The fumes of the chloroform filled her head. Making her dizzy. But that wasn't stopping Amanda. This couldn't happen again; she couldn't let Bailey win. Amanda used all her strength to kick Shea in the crotch. Making him foil over and drop to the floor. She then ran over to the gun, unstable and losing sight. She wrapped her hand around the pistol and aimed it at Bailey. But she didn't move. She kept her arms folded and her smile put. Amanda tried to pull the trigger. But the darkness overcame her body and crashed to the floor. Her eyes dropped weakly seeing Bailey become a blur. Then blackness. "Amanda, Amanda, Amanda..." Bailey tutted, then walked over to her body and placed her foot on top of her "When will you learn."

Jacob's eyes slowly opened. But it wasn't the only thing that was awakening. Again, his awful persistent cough awoke, creeping up his throat. It won't end for him. It won't end. He tried to bend over and cough. But he was stuck. Why was he stuck? His Arms were stuck. His legs. His chest. He was sitting down but trapped. His vision was sneakily creeping back. Bold lights reflected in his eyes, making him parsley blind. But his pupils adjusted. Everything was becoming clear. He looked down to see brown leather straps buckled around his chest, wrists, and legs. Was he strapped to a chair? He then coughed more. He saw small parts of his own blood sprawl out of his mouth as he coughed. His body was on fire. His throat was caged with thorns tightening around it and he was trapped. "Aww, is wee Jacoby sick? " A voice echoed. He looked around the forbidden room. The once-white walls, the grubby floor, and the one light hanging by one wire, flickering. But where was that voice?

Suddenly, just on the right of him a hand touched his shoulder and made its way up to his face, Bailey walked round and stood in front. Now holding his chin. Jacob didn't gasp, he was shocked. But he remained inside. It was her. It was really her. "Miss me?" she smiled "Not even for a second" Jacob replied, glaring at her. "Hmph" she laughed through her nose "Thought so" She then let go of his chin, making it flop. Suddenly a soft cough was voiced around the room. Right next to Jacob sat Amanda, in the same chair he was. Strapped. She groaned and pulled her head up slowly opening her eyes. "Ames!? You alright!?" "Oh. My sweet, sweet Amanda! My little freak! Are you okay?" Bailey mocked with a voice "Ugh. Makes me sick" Amanda then looked down and her eyes widened. She started pulling her wrists, her legs and pushing her chest forward. She was freaking out. "Where am I!?" she shrieked Bailey then laughed at her panicked emotion and folded her arms. "The place you stupidly came to. My place. My trap" "Let us go, Bailey!!" Amanda shouted "It's so cute that you think I'm just going to let you go so easily? God. I thought you were smart" "You don't have to do this. You can let us go and live your life! No harm, no prison. Just let us go and nothing will happen" "Live my life!?" She growled "Live my life!? My life has never been sunshine and rainbows, I dedicated my life to finding Jacob and you came along! You ruined it. You are the bitch that killed my father. You are the bitch that threw me behind bars! Do you know what's that like?" "No. Because we aren't psychotic like you" Jacob spoke. "You made me crazy!" Bailey looked at Jacob "You created this" "Then what!? What do you want from us!?" Amanda yelled, growing with anger. Suddenly the rusty door in front, with one small square window, squeaked open. Two men stepped inside. One man, they both knew. "Jason!?" Amanda said, so shocked and used. "God. These reactions are priceless. You guys really are dumb cops" Bailey laughed, cackling. "You work for her?" Jacob questioned "I don't work for her" Jason gritted, shutting the door "She is my sister" "Sister?" Amanda spoke, "She never mentioned you?" 'That's because I keep myself, to myself. But Tay here made me a deal. So, I am here to help and get what I want" "What do you mean, get what you want?" "That story will be told later" Bailey cut in "What took you so long anyways? Did you take care of the little girl and the brunette?" she said now turning to Jason. "Sorry that I had to make two stops. Plus, it wasn't easy finding the second place and breaking in. It is miles away and yes. They were dealt with" Jason replied. "Whatever. If the job is done" She rolled her eyes "Shea, did you search them?" "Like you asked." Shea then slapped two guns, broken radios, and phones on the tray next to them. A type of tray that will have operating tools. Small blades, scissors, pliers. But lucky enough. Nothing was on it. He then lifted out the orange tube with the painkillers.

"Ahh yes. Jason's little experiment" Bailey smiled "I see it's been working" Jacob then looked at her, who was smirking. He then looked down at the pills, something didn't feel right. She knew what they were and was happy. It all then clicked. Those weren't painkillers. Certainly not. Why else would she be smiling? "Amanda. How many did you have of them!!?" he shot his head at her "I-I don't know-" "How many!!!?" "M-Maybe Four? Three? I don't know Jacob. What's going on!?" Amanda then began coughing. Becoming more violent. She then suddenly scrunched up her face. Amanda tasted something questioning. She spat out her saliva. She looked down to see it was mixed with a pinkish color. Amanda lost her control. She gasped. That shouldn't be there. Everything seemed so wrong Her breathing became heavy. Her mind was drowning in fear. Her body shook, she went weak. "What's happening to me!!?" She cried, coughing a little again "What are those pills!!?" "My own design," Jason said so calming, stepping forward "A drug. Battling your immunity, your white blood cells. Killing all your strength your body holds. A sickness" he then picked the pills up and tossed one into his hand and placed it in between his index finger and thumb. "Killing you by stages" "Aww... Amanda, I almost feel bad for you" Shea replied sarcastically Amanda said nothing but looked at Jacob. Realizing that his zombie look was the pills affecting him. The coughing. The temperatures. The blood. They were dying by the second and they were both blind. "How could you do this!? You can't kill us!" Amanda cried, then looked down at his hand. His ring "You have a wife, Jason! Don't do this! Please!!" "DID!" Jason snapped "Past tense! Gone! Dead! Forgotten! Did have a wife!" he then walked over to Amanda and placed his two hands on the arms of the chair and leaned in close to her face "And it's made me stronger, stronger than before. Stronger than you. Your pleading isn't going to stop me" "Jason..." Amanda said softly, crying. He let his grip release from the chair and stood up, turning his back. "You've had more than just three pills. Placed one in little Jacob's coffee the first time we met. In your beer at the bar, and I'm guessing you believed it being paracetamol, so you do the math" "How" Jacob spoke ignoring what he last said, and his voice echoed "How did she die" Jason froze. Like his mind soaked up the words, collecting his memories and anger. Shea then spoke. "That's enough! We are asking you the questions. Not the other way around. Now shut the fuck up, before I shove the whole bottle of pills down your throat!" "Woah. Easy tiger. Let him speak" Bailey said. "Killed. I killed her" Jason provoked. Silence awoke. Nothing was said. "April. She didn't love me. She couldn't give me the one thing I wanted. She loved someone else. A cop." He said in disgust "Clearly I wasn't good enough. A cheater she was. She didn't know how good she got it. I wanted a family, that's all I asked. But she was weak" he inhaled. "So, I showed her what it would be like to be backstabbed. Literally." "Story gives me chills all the time" Bailey smiled. "But that's all going to change now, isn't little brother?" "Indeed" He grinned "To my readings. Jacob here seems to be ahead with the sickness. Stage two. The coughing stage, blood and weakness, and greyness of the skin. Stage one starts off with a simple cold. But stage two is intense" "What-" Jacob coughed and wheezed "What's stage three?" Amanda was shocked, she couldn't control her fear. They were dying by the second. But she was surprised that Jacob seemed to be keeping a stern face. He didn't seem scared. He looked brave. But she knew deep down inside that he was scared, just like her. "Dehydration. Sickness, more coughing. Unable to breathe at parts and stage four?" he smirked "I'll leave that for a surprise" "There must be something that could stop this!?" said Amanda "God. You are right. She is whiney" Shea scoffed. "Yes. There is. But here's the deal" Jason paced backwards and forwards "On my journey, I made a little stop. Your apartment" he glared at Amanda "And I couldn't help but to find something. Something that is all I wanted. A baby maybe?" Amanda gasped as he then pulled out her pregnancy test, the white and blue stick. So clear in the light "Ames... What is he talking about?" Jacob stammered She couldn't find the words. She was scared, surprised and shocked. She couldn't speak "Aww... Did Little Santiago does not tell you?" Jason pouted "There is an antidote. But, you can only have it in one condition" He paused, looking at the two cops. They didn't say a word. "Marriage." he said in glee, yet in a villain tone "You Jacob, marry my sister and Amanda, little Amanda Santiago, I want us to be the family I've always wanted. But that starts with you to marry me-" "HELL NO, YOU MONSTER!" "Then I guess you'll just die then, the same with your husband. Or should I now say? Friend" Bailey laughed and opened a piece of paper and showed it to Jacob and Amanda. A divorce document. Both their names are written down. The reason why they needed Sophia. The lawyer. "Sign it and you'll live" she glared. Amanda looked at Jacob, shaking her head and crying. Pleading him. Begging. She didn't want to die. But she didn't want to be split from the love of her life. "Fine" Jacob spoke "I'll sign it-" "Jacob, No! Please! You can't really be considering this!!?" "There is no other choice, Amanda! I can't let you die!" he sighed, now crying. He broke "Just trust me on this. Please?" Amanda looked at him. He trusted him. They will find a way... She hopes. "Okay," she said softly with her tears "I trust you," Jacob then nodded and looked back at Bailey. "If I sign this. We get the antidote?" "Correct and you'll be mine," she said in glee. Jacob took one more look at Amanda and sighed. He then looked at the sheet and the pen Bailey was holding. He nodded. She smiled and moved her head in a jester for Shea to untie his one hand. He took the pen. Signed it right on the bottom of the page. Bailey snatched back the paper and smiled down at him "You made a smart choice Jacoby," She then went over to Amanda and held it in front. She looked at it. Her eyes were flooding with tears. She couldn't believe it. She looked at her husband one last time for reassurance. He just smiled. Amanda took a deep breath and took the pen, scratching the ink onto the paper. It was done. "Perfect" Jason grinned and lifted out two small glass tubes filled with a clear liquid. The antidotes "You'll get these after the wedding" "You're seriously placing a wedding!?" Amanda Shouted "Yes" he smiled and now went to the door "Oh and don't worry. Your friends are invited as well. Shea?" he called "Keep an eye on them two" "Well not like I have a choice" "Friends!? What did you do!!!?" Jacob called. But the door was shut. They were sinking deep into doom.

Chapter 11: Say What?

The room Jacob and Amanda were stuck in, was grim. It wasn't Pleasant. The walls were seeped with greenery and the smell was also not welcoming, wasn't appealing to breathe in. They both sat in their chairs, eyes feeling heavy and almost dozing off as weakness held onto them and grew increasingly worse. But fear kept them awake. Amanda's throat felt like a blazing fire eroding with every cough she took. Her mind was a haze and her hunger crept on her slowly. Jacob, on the other hand, looked drowned in his own sweat. His face was glazed with his own sticky fluid and the bright light above, gave his face a glossy shine. He was burning up like a turkey. His mouth was dry like the Sahara Desert, desperate for the clench of thirst. Never had the craving for water before and just like Amanda, his cough overtook his body and controlled him.

They sat there for maybe, estimating, 25 minutes in their own silence and thoughts. Jacob had many. His mind was swimming, so much had happened. So much to think about. How to escape and when? What about the squad? They are in danger. But the one thing that was first played on his mind was the girl sitting next to him. Amanda. She was pregnant He was now going to become a Dad. He didn't know what to think of it. He didn't know where to start. But why didn't she tell her? How long did Amanda hide it away from him? "Why didn't you say?" Jacob rasped, it's the only thing they said between the 25 minutes of nothing "Say what?" Amanda questioned, her voice soft Jacob didn't respond immediately, instead, he looked at her with pitying eyes. Struggling to say, "Your pregnancy" He paused again "Our baby" Amanda's face dropped into a sad guilty look. She sniffed and looked down. "I was afraid" she answered "Afraid? Afraid of what?" "Of you, Jacob" Amanda said, not mad but softly "I know you are still not ready" Jacob didn't say a word.

He left Amanda's words back in the silence. It was like he was processing what she said, in fact, he was. "I am" Jacob finally spoke "I am afraid. I never had a Dad. I had to learn things on my own. I taught my-

self how to shave, ride a bike, and even get girl advice from my Mom."
He inhaled, shaking his head in slight anger "He wasn't there for me.
So, who do I look up to for father's advice?" But again, silence swallowed the room. But Jacob wasn't finished "But I'll be the better person, the better Dad" He then looked at Amanda "I'll be the Dad who
will be there for our kid. I'll teach her or him how to ride a bike, play
catch. We'll even watch die-hard movies on repeat, make them learn
all the lines. Cause I'm not going to leave them or you, Amanda" He
then smiled "I'm afraid, but I will never leave" Amanda laughed and
cried happy tears. She wanted to hug him so badly. But she couldn't.
They were trapped and strapped (Title of their sex tape). The speech
Jacob gave her, gave Amanda hope. They will escape. They will find
a plan. But suddenly a cackling laugh shambled in the room. "GOD!
That must be the sappiest thing I have ever heard," Shea laughed "Don't
you get it? That child now belongs to Jason. He is one crazy man looking for a family" "No" Amanda's voice grew "It's not his and never will
be" "Fine, suit yourself" Shea rolled his eyes and went back onto his
phone "Why?" Jacob called Shea looked up, now detached from social
media, and gave Jacob a look in disgust.

"Why what?" He asked dryly, waving his phone about. "Why are
you here?" He then smiled, laughed. Shea set down his phone and fixed
himself on his seat. Like he was ready to give a speech. Which he was. "I
want to help Bailey, get her revenge and mine" he started "All on Amanda." he then turned his gaze to her "Do you know what it is like to be
locked behind bars for four years!? Seeing your life fly away and burn!
I didn't have a phone for four years! Do you have any idea!?" "No," she
said obliquely "I am a cop. Not a criminal" "She threw you behind bars,
so what? That's your own cause" "That's not all the story" he said calming "Back in school, life was great. I was once friends with Ashley, we
got along. Well, didn't that just fall apart? Your little rat here decided
to join the group, pushing me away. You took her away from me! I was
left in the dirt! Forgotten!" he then paused and shook his head ruthless-

ly." Then I lost her for good. She moved schools. Never saw her again" "This is stupid!!" Amanda yelled "You want to cause pain because I was once friends with Ashley!? Listen to yourself! You are crazy! You guys were friends that's all in the past-" "I fucking loved her!" Shea blurted. Jumping to his feet. His face was red with anger. So much rage. But she ran his hand through his hair, inhaled, and continued. "But there is nothing you can do to fix that. Nothing. That's why I want you to know what it feels like to lose someone who you love for good" "Wow... Bailey and him are like crazy twins..." Jacob muttered under his breath to no one. "But you can fix it" Amanda spoke. Brows frowned. Her words made Shea freeze. "Shea, you can have that back. You don't have to do this. You don't have to be involved. You're free now, so why go back?" she paused, hoping to get across to him "You can see Ashley again, be friends. If you stay on Bailey's side... You'll make things worse," Shea's eyes still drilled onto the floor. It was almost like he was taking her words into consideration as his stern face began to drop into realization. Maybe she did get across to him. Broke him. Affecting him. Shea rose to his feet and started walking slowly, almost swinging his legs. She watched his face grow into a smile. He then stopped right at her. "You know..." he said Horsley, picking up the pills next to him on the tray "I don't think you have had enough of these... Cause all I hear is BULL-SHIT!" Suddenly Shea gripped Amanda's face, trying to shove the blue pill in her mouth. But she refused, she couldn't possibly let that happen. Not on her watch.

Amanda then pursed her lips together as tight as she could and threw her head left and right, trying to escape his grip, breathing heavily through her nose She then couldn't breathe. He pinched her nose to shut, blocking her only open-air ways. Now she had no choice but to open her mouth. If she didn't. Chances are she will pass out. There is no winning. "Let her GO!!" Amanda heard Jacob shout. But Shea didn't bite back. Not at all. He maintained his grin, still forcefully attacking Amanda. Her lungs were now in desperate need of oxygen, tightening around her chest. Making her choke on nothing. The sudden sound of her heartbeat swelling in her ear began to slow. Thump...Thump...Thump. She needed to breathe. She needed to. There was no other choice. Amanda released the pressure on her small lips and gasped, letting a pool of air fill her lungs once again. The feeling was rejuvenating. But all fear crashed back on her again. Something round was shoved into her mouth and forced to a close. She lost. It was the pill.

"Now swallow" He threatened "How dumb do you think I am? I don't listen to cops-" "Shea." A sudden voice awoke He turned round to see Bailey standing at the old, rusty metal door. Arms folded and looked annoyed. She always does. Shea rolled his eyes, something he likes to do a lot, and stood tall. He took one last look at Amanda, who now spat out the pill that bounced onto the floor, and narrowed his eyes. Shea turned his body round to his name. "What?" He replied bitterly "I specifically asked for you to keep an eye on them. Not torture them. We all know that's my job" "Bailey, listen. I get you are all little Miss Badass, but I am pretty sure, I, a fully grown adult, can also take care of a manipulative rat. Okay?" She looked at him and smiled. But we all know her smiles don't mean a damn thing. She pulled her head down and walked over to Shea. She laughed through her nose and placed her one hand on his shoulder. "Shea" she smiled again, inhaling the musty air. He then realized that the grip around his shoulder was sore. Too sore. She then pulled him forward "When I ask you to do something. You abide by my rules. Got it?" "Whatever-" Bailey's grip tightened even more, making Shea wince and slightly groan. "I'll say it again. Got it?" "Yes! Yes! Now get the hell off me!" Shea pulled his shoulder back and maintained eye contact with the blue-eyed blonde who was also looking at him.

Rage bubbled inside him. How embarrassing to look so weak in front of the two cops. He wanted to be the person in charge, in the lead. But he knew that was Bailey's throne. She was tough, for sure, but her madness was worse. "Get out. I need to handle something. Go find Jason" Shea huffed like a kid and dug his hands into the pockets of his jacket, lifting his phone and leaving. Bailey then grabbed one of the chairs and flipped it on reverse. She sat down and put her arms over the head of the chair. "Reminds me of the good old times, doesn't it Santiago?" Amanda said nothing, but just glared while coughing. It was no use to entertain her. She learned that. She then watched her pick up Jacob's phone, observing it. She pushed the button on the bottom of the phone, which awoke the screen. In front of her eyes sat Jacob's wallpaper. The couple. Jacob and Amanda. Disgusting, she hated it. Always about her, the neat freak. The Nerd. "Cute wallpaper you got here, Jacoby," she said sarcastically "But let's spruce it up, shall we?" Bailey unlocked the camera icon and went over to Jacob. She placed her lips onto his and stretched out her arm. In one click the photo was taken. Amanda was filled with rage. "Better!" she said with such glee, now setting it as a wallpaper "Now to the real reason..." Bailey unlocked his phone. No passwords. Perfect. A real Jacob moves. She then clicked on Jacob's messages and found the name, captain. Of course, Jacob Nicknamed him Captain Dad. She began to type, her smile increasing more. The sounds of the keyboard tapping were faint in the room. Then it was sent. "Looks like no one will be suspecting a thing" She laughed "Your little father figure is going to think you two heroes found the little girl and have everything sorted. Of course, you guys will be running a little late for your beach house vaccination. So, I just had to let him know."

Jacob then asked. "How do you know about that?" "Jason. He is my eyes and ears." They both had nothing to say. Everything was crumbling into pieces like a biscuit. Little by little. They were getting weaker by the second and their friends were in danger. Bailey then threw the phone on the floor and crushed it with her heel. "Oopsie" she grinned "Guess you don't need that anymore" Bailey then pulled out a gun from the back of her belt. Pointing it at Jacob "Now, what I want you to do. Is get out of this chair. And purpose" "You can go to hell for all I care-"

Bailey placed the muzzle on his forehead. Digging it in. "You'll do what I say!" she then unbuckled the straps of his chair "Get down on your knees and purpose" She then pulled out a ring from her black jeans. Jacob looked at Amanda, who was worried sick for him. But there was nothing she could do. He had to listen to her rules. Jacob looked back up at her and the cold silver muzzle glaring at him. He sighed deeply, took the ring, and went down on one knee. The muzzle was back on his forehead. He could feel its chill. "Now say it" she almost spat. "Bailey..." he took one last look at Amanda, who was now crying. It broke him. But he can't do anything. He was too weak. Even leaning on his one leg made him feel woozy. He then looked at the ring "Will- will you marry me?" Bailey's smile creased more. She held her hand as he slid it on her finger, regretting those horrible words. "Yes, Jacoby." she then held up her hand. Looking at the jeweled stone "I will marry you," Jacob looked at the floor.

He could feel Amanda's pain and hear her soft crying. He wanted to go home. He wanted to sit on the couch and watch movies with her. The normal times. The safe moments. But here they are. Marrying a couple of crazy nut jobs. He then felt her hand wrap around his arm and being pulled up to his feet. Without a notice. She placed her lips forcefully onto his. God, he hated it. He hated it so much that he pulled away. But all she did was lick her lips and grin. "Now. What's going to happen is that you two are going to be placed in a room. From there, you can have your beauty sleep. After all," she giggled "Tomorrow we are going on a little trip and it's a very big day!" Bailey then pulled Jacob's arms together and pushed them up his back, placing the gun on the back of his head. "Now start walking." Bailey shoved him forward, opening the door and pushing him out. Behind, he can hear Amanda calling his name and squirming in her chair. Still strapped. Suddenly Jason appeared in front, also armed with a pistol. He pointed it directly at him as Bailey pushed Jacob to him. "Take him to one of the rooms. Make sure it's locked properly. Don't want anything happening like last time. Got it?" Jason nodded and took Jacob by his arms. Placing the gun to his back. His feet slapped the concrete, the dark musty concrete. Trying to stall time. He didn't want to be locked away; he didn't want to leave Amanda alone. But he couldn't stop, his head couldn't process what to do next. He was losing hope. Maybe this was it for them Jacob then bent over coughing, falling to his knees. His weak body couldn't take anymore. He felt sick, a vomit sick. This wasn't good. What stage was he on?

"Get up." Jason pulled at him. Yanking Jacob to his knees. He then came to a stop at a room. Inside, it was clear it was a room for the crazy. For the unstable. It had only one bed, where the mattress was heaped with mold. No sheets. No nothing. The power still worked, surprisingly. As a dim light above was on. Jacob was thrown in, falling to his knees. He wanted to fight so much, but he couldn't. He just can't. The door clattered to a shut, echoing down the hallway. "Don't-" Jacob inhaled, hard to breathe "Don't touch her" he called to Jason still standing at the door where he looked through a small winnow. "Don't worry about her...She'll be fine"

Next morning arrived. Vacation time. Drinking time and celebration. A time when the squad all gather up and loosen up, have fun, and split some jokes. Terry pulled one of her black bags over her shoulder and was waiting outside her apartment building. Her bag was filled enough for only three nights. She didn't need much. Ashley, on the other hand, struggled to carry her three bags of suitcases down the stairs. Three. Terry heard her groan in stress and saw her struggle. She didn't even have to look behind her to know what was happening. She was well aware that Ashley, without a doubt, had over-packed. Why wouldn't she? It's her. She sighed dropped her slightly dense bag rolled her eyes and spoke. "Ashley. We've been over this. You don't need three bags" "Terry, babe. Come on. I need one for my liquor, another one for clothes, duh, and the last one for my skincare and phone stuff. So yes. I do need three bags" she smirked. "Whatever give me the-" Just as Terry picked up one of her suitcases, she exhaled so much air. It was strangely heavy "Are you sure you didn't pack rocks!?" she gasped, slamming it down. "Hey! Easy gurl! That's my liquor you got there. Mama knows that wasn't cheap" She flicked her hair and set her sunglasses on her face that were previously on top of her head. Just suddenly, Terry arrived outside with his classic minivan. Ashley scoffed, pulling her sunglasses down slightly, and looked at Terry. "If you really think I am getting in that, you're wrong," Just then, Boyle rolled down his window in the back seat. "Hey there beach pals! I Brought snacks!" he smiled, showing tubs of whatever the hell it was sitting within it. Let's just say, it didn't look edible. Ashley didn't even want to know what it was. "Especially next to that. Pass," she replied, pushing her glasses fully up and turning her body around, and began to walk back. But Terry grabbed the hood of her hoodie and jolted her back. Dragging her into the car as she huffed on the way. After a while of struggling to place Ashley's bags in the minivan. They were set. Already on the road. The beach house was a few miles away. So, it was going to be quite a trip. A long trip for Ashley as she sat next to Boyle, slurping and munching on his weird concoction he made for his so-called 'Snacks'. "Terry. Tell Boyle to stop slurping in my ear. It's annoying," "Oh yeah? You think you have it bad? I'm currently sitting next to Scully and Hitchcock. Can you tell them to stop manspreading!?" Terry shouted from the back of the car. "I'm going on this vacation to escape from my kids. Turns out I was placed back with big ones! I am not your father. Sort it out yourself" Terry said, gripping the wheel.

The car journey was long. There were complaints. Toilet breaks and an hour of Ashley blasting Beyoncé. But all came to an end. They finally reached the house. It was just by the beach, it sat beautifully. It was a vibrant bold white house, very modern. They all smiled, excited to start the fun. Along came another car, holt. He preferred to drive on his own, which was a smart idea. Everyone was hopping out of their car, collecting their stuff, and approaching Holt. "Jacob and Amanda on their way?" Terry asked. "I got a message from him last night. They will be running a bit late. I suppose we should just go inside and wait for them. Theoretically, they shouldn't be long," "Let's get this party straightened," Ashley cheered, pointing her fingers to the sky and skipped to the door. She was immediately greeted by a tray of champagne glasses, sitting on the unit right next to the door. She didn't hesitate to grab it. No second thoughts. "Don't mind if I do," she sang lifting the glass and sipping at it. Walking in and turning her body to see everyone else coming in. Grabbing a glass. "Nice gesture Boyle" Terry added. Drinking away. "I didn't set this up?" he said, but no one really listened. As per usual. "To a great night coming!" Terry spoke, raising her glass, as everyone else did, and repeated "To a great night!" They all took a pause to drink the remaining inside of the small champagne glasses. It tasted so lovely and smooth, so rich in flavor. "Hey," Ashley called from the living room "Look at what I found," Everyone turned their gaze to Ashley who held up a beige envelope in the air. The squad, well, part of the squad, made their way towards her and all stood behind Ashley.

"Well, what is it?" Holt asked so monotone. "No idea" Ashley replied "Oh! I bet it's a discount for wing sluts! We hit the jackpot buddy!" Scully said to Hitchcock. But they were wrong, they were all so wrong. Ashley opened the envelope to a card. Not any card. One that was shocking. They didn't know what to say. Was this all part of the plan? "A wedding?" Boyle questioned, taking the card "But Jacob and Amanda are already married?" "I don't get it," Ashley said as she watched Terry snatch the paper. She opened it fully, scanning her eyes over the words. No. No. What she was reading can't be true. Right? This was all a joke, she thought. This was a prank. It must be the reason why Jacob and Amanda aren't here yet. This is a fraud. Ashley looked at Terry. She knew something was up. "What does it say?" Ashley asked.

"Dear nine" Terry read "You are all officially invited to Jacob and Amanda's wedding, in addition to Amanda marrying Jason," She paused long and hard, sharpening her eyes on one of the names "And the other, Jacob and Bailey," She looked up to see everyone's face's drop. They didn't know what to believe. Is this all true? Terry continued. "We look forward to seeing you. So, drink up. Cause soon it's going to be a special day" she finished, slowly looking up. Her heartbeat thumped against her chest. Things were so terribly wrong. She then looked at all the empty glasses everyone was holding. It clicked. "We need to get out of here, now!!" Terry shouted, flinging the card and grabbing her leather jacket. "Don't let your eyes close!" She spun her body around, but suddenly felt a bit hazy. Her mind seemed to become a blur, along with her vision. Every step she tried to take felt like her feet were blocks of cement. Her body went limp, bones feeling like jelly, and she fell to her knees. "We-" she started, but then her speech became slurred "We-need to get ouzo." Terry becomes more and more hazed. Tired. Behind her Ashley held her head, trying to shake off the funny feeling. As was Holt. Now sitting down on one of the sofas, as for Hitchcock and Scully? It didn't take them long to finally be passed out together. Ashley slowly slid down to the floor, woozy. Her eyes refused to stay open. She couldn't possibly control herself. "Terry... I... I can't keep them open" she whispered, almost like she was losing her voice. But Terry was already passed out on the floor. Eyes closed. Quietly snoozing. Holt was out too, lying on the sofa unconscious. Ashley then took one last look at the wedding card and sighed. "There better be cake..." And just like that, her head flopped to her shoulder, and passed out. Once again, Bailey was always one step ahead.

Chapter 12: Just Like That

Amanda squirmed on her chair, crying for Jacob's name. She wanted him beside her, she didn't want him to leave. God knows what could happen. She shouted so much that she could feel herself lose her voice. Every time she shouted felt like small stones scrapping her esophagus. The pain was sharp. Amanda decided to give up, lowering her head and weeping. God, how much she missed her apartment already, sitting down with Jacob, watching movies while she would cuddle up next to him. She only wishes and dreams for it now. "Stop your crying already" Bailey came walking in, high-heeled boots clacking on the ground. "It doesn't look pretty" Bailey then unbuckled the brown straps around her ankles, wrists, and chest, the ones Keeping her captive. Bailey then pulled her by the arm, yanking Amanda to her feet. But she couldn't tackle it. Her body wasn't in the right state to have the own strength to stand on her own two feet. Amanda was now powerless, falling to her knees. "Oh, for god's sake," Bailey groaned, pulling her back up "I'm not doing everything for you, now get over it and walk on your own two feet" Amanda bent over, hands on her knees and coughed. She then looked up, glaring at her. "God" Amanda laughed "I wish to put ten bullets through your head," Bailey growled, gritting her teeth. Oh, how that made her so infuriated. She then grabbed her face, pulling it up to eye level, and brought out her knife that always sits at the side of her hip, Always, and brought it to her throat. "And you don't think that I don't fantasize about me cutting you right here!?" she vexed in fuming rage, shaking Amanda's face at the same time. "Cause trust me wee doll, make me snap?" She sinisterly laughed "You'll know exactly where this will be going" She shined her knife right at her throat. Amanda didn't dare to gulp. Bailey pushed Amanda's face away from her, stepping back, still having the knife in her hand, and looked right at her. But Amanda said nothing. Instead, she just stood weakly, rubbing her throat. Coughing. "Your silence is music to my ears," Bailey smiled "Now hands behind your back," She now held out a gun. This woman was loaded. But Amanda didn't process her words. She was too busy drowning in her own fear of what to do next. She heard her clearly. But her mind didn't abide. "I said put your fucking hands behind your back!!!" She spat, jabbing the gun in the air at her. And just like that, Amanda's brain snapped, following her rules. Discreetly placing her two hands behind her. "Good" She then Went over forcefully grabbing her wrists and pushed her forwards. Amanda felt the metallic muzzle of the gun pinch her back, almost making her hair perk up with fear. She was shoved out of the door and into the dark grim hallways. It was still dark outside. But what time was it? All she knew was that tomorrow when the sun was up. That was a day that was supposed to be their vacation time. Not anymore. Suddenly Jason came walking down, glaring at Amanda with a proud grin, almost like he was saying she was mine. It was that type of look. "Want me to take her?" He asked his sister. "No, I have a special room that I know she would love to stay in" Amanda, Jason, and Bailey continued to walk down the halls, the gun still forcefully poking her back. Something in the back of her head was screaming for her to grab the gun. Grab it! Grab it! You'll be free! Kill her and escape! But Amanda isn't the type of person to kill. No chance. But in this situation, it was turning her personality. Making her go insane. Making her want to put the gun to her head, put her finger on the trigger, and BLAM! That would be it. Gone. Dead.

No more Bailey. As for Jason? She hasn't built too much hate for him, yet. Is he insane like his sister? Yes. But she was mad. A lunatic.

A demon needing to be put to sleep. Just as her thoughts swiped away. Amanda noticed that they stopped at a door. Jason in front opened the door, creaking so painfully. There it was. That room. That horrible grim room. It brought back too many memories. "Welcome home," Bailey said "Home, sweet, home-" Bailey got cut off. She did it. Amanda built the courage to turn her body as quickly as she could and grab the pistol. It was that easy. Ooh, how Amanda smiled, placing the muzzle on her head. "Give me two reasons why I shouldn't put a full round of bullets, right through that sick head!!!" Amanda shouted. Jason behind pulled out his weapon. But Bailey raised her hand out to him. "No, don't," She assured him calmly, then placing her eyes back onto Amanda "Go ahead. Do it," She then grabbed the muzzle, placing it on her forehead "Pull the trigger Ames" Amanda stalled. Why was she stalling? Right now, she could be free. But something held her back. She isn't a killer. Amanda is not a killer. "Go! Pull it! Pull the trigger!" Bailey repeated, now forcing the muzzle on her head harder. "Tay..." Jason spoke. "Shut it, Jason," she snapped "Do it, Amanda. Or are you too weak?" "I'm not weak..." Amanda said meekly. "Then do it," Amanda put more pressure on the trigger, her skin molding into the weapon. She was thinking about everything she had done. Everything Bailey did ruined her. Scarred her for life. Finally. Rage took over her. Infuriating rage took over control. "Enjoy hell, you bitch!" And just like that, she pulled the trigger. Wincing in anticipation. Click. Amanda opened her eyes. Nothing happened. Why didn't it work? Click, click, click She pulled again. But nothing. The chamber was empty. Bailey played her. "Pathetic" she smiled taking the gun and kicking her in the stomach that made her fall into the room. Amanda fell hard on her back, winded. Gasping for air. She groaned, holding her chest and rolling on the floor. All she could hear was Bailey laughing. "Aww" she giggled again "You really thought I would let you do that?" she sneered, reloading her gun "You're right. Cops are dumb," She then pulled out a box of cigarettes, flicked the flap open, and pulled out the stick of addiction, plac-

ing it in her mouth. "I'm away for a smoke. In the meantime? It's best
you get some sleep, hero," And just like that, Bailey walked away. Amanda was shocked, lying on the floor just utterly shocked. She got played
like a fool. A dumb cop. Jason then stepped inside, crouching down to
his knees, and putting his fingers on her chin. "Don't take it too per-
sonally" he smiled "She likes to play a lot of games" "I noticed" Amanda
replied bitterly.

"Don't worry about it. You'll get used to it eventually" "Used to it?"
"Yeah. Me, you, and little Jacob, and Bailey. One big family" he paused,
then putting a hand on her stomach "And our little baby" Amanda shuffled her body away from him in anger. "To hell if you think you are going to be the father" "I don't think you have a choice in that Ames" He
stood to his feet "You're now in my control" "Do you see a ring on this
finger?" Amanda replied sarcastically. At least she still had some of that
left. But Jason just smirked. "Oh, there soon will be" He then leaned
his body against one of the walls in the room. Arms folded that tensed
his muscles. He did nothing but just look down, tensing his jaw. "Was
she always this crazy?" Amanda was tempted to ask. He then looked
up, taking a moment to process what she said, and inhaled through his
nose. Deeply. "No" he then spoke "She was once innocent" "What in
the hell created the crazy in her?" He stalled, looking the other way as
his head was turned showing his sharp jawline and his short-trimmed
beard. Again, he tensed his jaw, clamping it. "Rachel" He smiled "That
was her name. My mother" he shook his head "We were one happy
family. You know, like one of those pathetic TV adverts you see of
an American family? That was us. We did everything together" Jason
paused "But that all came crashing down. Hard. My father worked late
one night. He wasn't home at all. So, it was just me, Tay, and our Mom.
God," he laughed "We used to love it when she tucked us in bed. She
would read this book I had the minute I could walk. It never got old,"
He stopped almost like he could see the memory so vividly, just smiling while gazing at the floor. "But that one night, that only night Dad

wasn't there" He scoffed "It happened. A burglary. He broke into the house, knowing so little that Bailey and our Mom would still be up. An idiot he was. But she was so brave. So brave. The man decided to lift his gun," Jason then lifted his arm, modeling his fingers into a gun and jacket it. "Balm, one bullet, straight for Bailey. But as a mother, you would do anything for your child. Even risking your own life" he paused, processing his words "And she did. She risked it. Jumping right in front of young Tay. Dead center in the chest. And just like that, that small bullet caused a pool of blood. All I heard was screaming from my sister. Screaming for help. She didn't know what to do. Only 13 years old, holding her mother dying." He shook his head again. Licking his lips. But no tears, no tears at all. "My father blamed it all on her. All day long she was hated. A disappointment. It turned her. She hated anyone who would get in her way or steal anyone who she loved" Amanda looked at Jason. She felt sorry for him and Bailey. She had no idea. But still wasn't an excuse to be so insane to others. Right? "I'm sorry..." Amanda said in a slight whisper. "It's alright. Things happen for a reason" he said calmly Jason being nice? It was bizarre for Amanda to see him so calming. Maybe she could break him. Turn him into someone new. All she had to do was break him, like shea. He broke... Well, Sort of. "Do you ever visit her grave?" "Na" He shook "It killed me to see her alone. But I guess she is now buried with Dad."

"I'm sure she is proud- loves you. She loves you" she stuttered. "But not proud" "What do you mean?" He snapped. "Well... You did kill your wife. Do you think she would be proud of the son she raised, turning out to be a killer?" "She didn't love me!!" Jason snapped, throwing himself off the wall "She hated me!" "It doesn't mean that you had to kill her, Jason!" "What the fuck do you know!?" He vexed, grabbing her by the throat "You've never experienced hatred!! You have no idea what it's like!" He then let go, making her gasp and rub her neck. "No," she said weakly "I don't. But you do and you know what you did was wrong! You know murder isn't the answer! But you can change that. Make her proud. Jason, please. Don't let this happen. If you let us go-" "Let you go? Ha!" he chuckled "Listen. I don't want to play your little guilt game here. I know what you are doing, you think you can just break me like that? You think you can change me?" Amanda looked into his blue eyes with fear. Too smart he was. "Nobody can change. Not even Bailey. So don't even try," he then went to the door, opened it, and stopped "Not even me," The door slammed shut and Amanda was left alone with her thoughts. Sick and cold.

J ason stepped outside into the open. Outside was cold, dark but dry. To the left of him stood Bailey, resting her back on the bricked wall whilst having one foot upright on the wall as well. Next to her stood Shea. She kept her gaze ahead, puffing her cigarette, inhaling and exhaling. "What took you so long," she said, not even turning her head. Jason dug his hands into his pockets and walked over to her, resting his back on the wall. Looking up at the sky. "Talking a bit of sense into her. That's all" But she replied with nothing. Still puffing away, watching the smoke glide in the thin, crisp air like a clouded lake. He didn't smoke, not even in his teen years. His mother would always scare him into stories about the toxic cigarette. Of course, he was a mama's boy. He would listen to anything she said the only thing around them was now silence. It was nice. But something Jason never really liked. He didn't like to be left with thoughts. But thankfully Bailey broke it. "What's the plan for tomorrow?" "I've already got it set, by the time we get there. They should already be passed out" "What genius idea did you create?" she said, now turning to him and smiling. "Nothing special" he shrugged "Just a couple of drinks for a celebration, that's all" Bailey smirked, nodding her head and took a puff. Inhale, exhale. "I knew you wouldn't disappoint me," she said looking up to the sky. Again, she took another draw. Inhale, exhale. Shea, next to Bailey, was zoned out on his phone, like always. Jason didn't really like him, he seemed useless to him. Just someone who was slowing them down. Shea thought the exact same about Jason. They both hated their company. But it didn't matter. Bailey was the one in the lead. She didn't need to say it. You just knew. She has experienced more, been in the life of jail longer, and did I mention she is crazy?

Chapter 13: What Did They Do?

Hella crazy. But she once was an innocent little girl, before she hit her teen years. So gorgeous. Back then she smiled more, laughed more, and enjoyed life. Jason then laughed through his nose and spoke, breaking the night's quietness. "Remember that teddy you always carried around with you? What was it called again?" Bailey laughed herself "Snuffles?" "Ah! That's it, Snuffles," He chuckled "You always had to go everywhere with it" "Oh yeah? Remember that little night light you always had on because you were afraid of the dark? Probably still have it" Bailey teased, lifting her cig to her mouth. "Very funny, but those fears are long gone" He laughed along with Bailey. And just like that, night's silence snapped back. Again, Jason didn't like it. Must mute the thoughts. Silence the thoughts. Let's not think about the thoughts. What thoughts you must be wondering? His mind was scarred by the memories. April. His wife. Her smile was warm in his memories, her body so toned. Brunette and forest green eyes. But he can't think about her. He can't. He turned his gaze to Bailey. Whisking the subject away "She loves you. You know that, right?" Bailey looked down at her brother. She knew exactly who he was talking about. She shot her gaze back to the sky ahead. "She died because of me," She replied bluntly "You were thirteen Tay," "Yeah, old enough to save her," "There was nothing you could do. Forget what Dad said-" "What he said is true!" She snapped, now looking at him "I haven't even got my life planned out! I spent most of my years training as a police officer to get to the person I love, then what? End up behind bars in the end? I didn't have anyone who loved me, Jason. They all turned their backs on me for someone else! Just like you and Dad!" She grew with anger." You may be here now. But I had to buy you to get you here. You left me, like everyone else. So don't stand here before me trying to go all soft about Mom. Do you really think she would be proud of us? I mean, just look at us!" she then flicked her cigarette to the floor and crushed it with her heeled boot" It's time to wake up Jason. This is reality" Bailey stormed off, back into the gloom building, leaving Jason outside with Shea. He expected her to react, but not that bad. He sighed, pinching his eyes in disparity. He tried to clear the words out of his head. His mom is proud...surely. He then looked up to see Shea smugly smirking at him "What are you staring at!? Shows over!"

Jacob didn't sleep at all. None. He couldn't possibly let his mind shut off, relax, and shut his eyes. Not when his mind was clogged with so many thoughts and fears. He was hungry, tired, and sick. So sick that it got to the point where he couldn't breathe at times and had a nose-bleed. He was now on stage three. No clue of what stage four is. Jacob didn't know what time it was, but it already felt like he was stuck in that room for a week. Now he really knows what it was like for Amanda. He couldn't stop thinking about her. Where was she? Was she safe? What did they do to her?

"Morning Jacoby" A voice called. Bailey stood at the door that was now open "Ready for a road trip?" Jacob, sitting on the floor, said nothing. Just looked at her with hate. "Hmm" she smiled "I'll take it as a yes" She then walked over and stopped. Scrunching up her face. "Oh... Jacoby. You really don't look so good" She then pulled out the antidote that sat in a small glass tube "Maybe I should give you this?" Jacob's eyes widened and his heart skipped a beat. Never has he pawned for something so much in his life that it gave him the energy to quicken to his feet. "Well, well, well. Look who just got his mojo back? Guess I'll put this away till after the wedding," she said, putting it back in her jeans. "You monster..." Jacob growled. Wanting to choke her so much "Your little monster" she teased poking his nose like a button. "Now let's go. Your friends are waiting" She then grabbed his wrists and tightened them with a zip tag. Pulling it as it got smaller around his wrists. He then got dragged out, down the ratchet hallways and outside. It was daylight, morning and the sun was still pale. He then got thrown into a car, in the back, and thumped onto a seat, next to him sat Amanda unconscious, also having a gag around her mouth. Wrists trapped. "Ames? Ames! Wake up!" he called "Amanda!?" "She is unconscious, Jacob" Jason called from the front "Take the hint" "What did you do to my friends? Tell me you didn't hurt them!" "I guess you'll find out," Bailey said, right next to him at the door "But for now? You can finally get some rest" She then wrapped his mouth around with a gag. But something smelt off about it. It smelt like toxic fumes, filling his nose. Wait. It was chloroform, he remembers the smell. Of course, it was, of course. Just then, Jacob's eyes began to drop. Getting heavier by the second. "You bit..." Jacob was then out cold. Out flat. The beauty of drugs, they come in so handy for those in the wrong hands. Very wrong hands. "Shea, jump in the back," Bailey said to him. "No, you jump in the back. I'll sit in the front" "I'm sorry. I forgot. Who makes the rules?" she threatened. Shea paused, sucking his teeth, and rolled his eyes. "Fine. Whatever," Shea jumped in the back, sitting in the middle between Jacob and Amanda. Heads lolling. Bailey jumped in the front, making the car slightly shake, and slammed the door shut. "Let's get going" And just like that. They were on the road. Driving their way to trouble. Everything they planned was going smoothly. They were always one step ahead. Always. Bailey didn't dare to slip up, not this time. She was always smart. Everyone expected her to be the dumb typical popular blonde. They were wrong. All those negative people were so incorrect. She wasn't organized like Amanda or nerdy, but she was quick-

thinking. Ahead of the game. This time, she will succeed. She will finally be with Jacob. It will happen. Jason will get the family he wants. Bailey will be with Jacob and Shea. Pet. He can do whatever. He knows his
plan. Hours passed. They came across many trees, cars, and traffic lights.
But they made it. They reached their checkpoint. Jason drove up to the
beach house discreetly. Ahead the house is so white and beautiful. It
was clear the squad was already there as cars were parked outside. Only
two. Bailey's lip curled into a smile, ready to begin something new. Jason jolted the car to a stop, making Shea jump in fear, now awake from
his slumber. Of course, he complained and groaned. But no one really
cared. They were too busy eying the house, forming plans A, B, and C
for anything that could go wrong. Like I said, Bailey was always ahead.
She didn't hesitate but to jump out of the car and go straight for the
door. The other can take care of the two detectives, or a now former
sergeant for Amanda. But Bailey was dedicated to taking the lead like
always. Be the alpha and bite the bullet. She kicked the door, but it was
already ajar, causing it to slam shut loudly. She raised her gun high. Just
in case. But there they were. All lying down on the floor, blacked out.
Seeming so lifeless. Champagne glasses sat on the table and an invitation card sat on the ground. It made her smile. "Let's get this fucking
wedding on the go..."

Chapter 14: All That Hate

Jason watched Bailey enter the house alone. She left him and Shea to deal with the two cops in the back, unconscious. Jason placed his head on the headrest of the car seat and groaned. So much to be done just to be with Amanda. His fiancée, the one who was carrying their child. That's right. Not Jacobs, his. Jason's child. It was going to be his, he will make sure of it. April wasn't the one for him, she didn't love him. She couldn't even produce a child. Weak she was. She needed to be let go. Forgotten. Right? But those forest green eyes and her soft luxurious chocolate oak hair were breathtaking. Her faint small little kisses of the sun, her freckles, were so beautiful. He remembered her so clearly. So vividly. That smile that made a rainy day better. "Why?" Jason's eyes widened. He knew that soft, smooth sweet caramel voice slithered into his ear like a soft waterfall. He lifted his head and gazed his eyes to the right. There she was. April. "Baby...I'm-" he said, so softly. But got cut off by her cotton voice "Why did you do it?" she began to tear up. Jason then noticed the bruising around her neck. So purple and red. Looking so painful to touch. It only made him realize that those terrible marks glaring at him, were the cause of his bare scandalous hands. Her face wasn't the beautiful warm coffee glow. It was pale. Her face was gaunt, so dead-looking. Whatever happened to her smile? "You didn't love me" He closed his eyes "You didn't love me, I had to do what was right," He then opened them to realize his first love was gone. Nothing was there. He did nothing but just stare at the empty seat she previously was in. Suddenly a held-back snigger was heard in the back from Shea, still currently in the car. Jason looked behind him and glared at him so devilishly. "I-um" He then vigorously pulled at the door handle "Why won't this DOOR WORRK" Suddenly Bailey came walking out of the beach house, strutting, with such a proud grin. Almost like she won something. Well, to be in fact. She won the battle against the nine-nine. "Bailey" Shea called, banging on the window "Jason's talking about his ghost of a girlfriend, and can someone please get the firkin keys for this damn door!" He continued to pull. She heard his muffled voice from inside the car and cringed. She took one glance at her brother, and he was sharply looking the other way. Bailey groaned, rubbed her face, and pulled the door handle, letting Shea spill out of the car. "Thank god, at least someone isn't wanting to screw ghost the girlfriend" He joked, then looked at Bailey who was looking at Jason "He's going soft Tay" He mumbled "Quiet!" She snapped "Go inside and tie everyone up to one chair each. Ropes are in the back of the car. Make sure they are tight, Understand? I'll be there in a second" She then flipped her eyes back to Jason "I need to sort something out," Shea looked at him as well and rolled his eyes. Pathetic. He was such a softie from his perspective. Who could like him? Certainly not shea. No. He hated him, Shea knew he was mentally stronger than him. Maybe not physically. But mentally. He groaned, turning his body around, and went to the trunk of the car, pulling out the heaps of ropes that looked like snakes. He placed them around his shoulder and strummed to the house. He had to do everything. Everything by Bailey's words, so demanding, so strict. She liked to be ahead; he knew that from their past friendship. She liked to be in charge, the alpha. The leader. But Shea wanted that more. He wanted to make her proud and seem bigger. They both shared something in common.

Hating Amanda. As he walked through the door, he met his eyes upon the nine, all passed out on the floor. Champagne glasses sitting about. Another thing of Jason's drug. That man seems to like his drugs.

Metaphorically. There were two old, hideously snoring men on the sofa at the back, along with a man on the other sofa who seemed so professional looking, even for being passed out. Shea was getting Gay vibes from him. Next to him, a man who was ripped, possibly muscles with muscles, wearing a robe and a fanny pack, was also passed out. I wonder how many walls he can punch through. Shea thought on the floor not so far from him, lay a woman with thick black curled hair, with a leather jacket. Even in her sleep, she somehow seemed to look like she wanted to kill someone. And just then, his eyes glanced at the one person who made his heart skip slightly. Ashley. It was her. So many years of not seeing her, there she was. Out on the floor, still holding her phone. Obviously. "Ashley, Ashley, Ashley" Shea taunted, walking over to Terry and going over to her, down on his knees "I'm sorry but there can only be one social media King" Shea then took her phone and unlocked it, opening to Twitter and sighed and laughed, looking back down at her. "You're so beautiful laying there with the newest iPhone" He tucked her hair and went back to her phone "Of course you're on Twitter leaving bad reviews on a chicken wing company. Ha! We have so much in common! This could've been so different I- I'm glad it's NOT" he laughed, stroking her face "Love you lots of Ashley queen but unfortunately today, Shae Knows Best" Shea was wildly happy. Maybe fangirling over her... Maybe. But all those years, he just looked up to her. Especially in high school. But when she wakes up? It's a whole new shea is going to meet...

Bailey jumped in the front of the car and slammed the door shut. "What?" Jason said bitterly "You need to let go" She kept her eyes to the front "You're becoming weak" "Weak?" "Yes, Jason" She replied bluntly "Weak. You're starting to go crazy" Jason clamped his jaw shut in anger. He couldn't say anything. He didn't like being called weak. 'Cause deep down he knows it's true. April was attacking his mind like a spreading disease. Developing and growing. The memories were getting bigger. "Let go of April, let go of everything! Even Mom! It's all in the past! See that nerd back there?" Jason looked back at Amanda still out cold. "That's your future now" She snapped "And there is no backing out now" Jason groaned and sighed. He wasn't going to back out. No. Amanda was perfect for him, she was beautiful. Maybe not April's limits. But still pretty. He looked at his sister, right at her blue eyes, and spoke. "Let's just get them inside"

Terry groaned, head feeling heavy like a big cement block. Her hair hung over her face like draped curtains, covering her sight. Her mouth felt dry but tasted rather unusual. Something sweet but sour. She couldn't remember a thing. Her mind was blank like a piece of paper. A sheet of white. Where was she again?

She groggily lifted her head, wincing at the light that hit her eyes. Nothing came to her mind. What happened? Terry flicked her hair and blew the strands away from her face. Her eyes adjusted and her mind finally began to work. She noticed that her arms were behind her, but not her back. A chair. She looked up to see she was sitting at the dinner table and not alone. Four more chairs sat ahead, three seats filled with Ashley directly across, Charles and Scully. They were tied, rope wrapped around their chest tightly and gags around their mouth. All still out cold. Just beside her sat Holt and Hitchcock. Also tied the same and flat out. She was the only one awake. Terry gave her hands a wiggle, feeling the zip tag caress her skin around her wrists and the rope push on her chest. Outside was becoming dark as the sun seemed to be dying off. How long was she out for? Terry turned her head to the left, looking into the lounge area with seats, and saw a fireplace lit. Everything just suddenly hit her like a ton of bricks. Her last memory was picked up, she remembered the invitation to a wedding and those champagne glasses. She remembered that name printed on the card.

Bailey. Her heart even pounded to the name, making her blood turn to ice. She needed to get out. "Ghana!" She muffled under her gag. But nothing, simply nothing. "Tay" A manly voice called "We've got one awake" Terry whipped her head to the left and saw- wait- no, it can't be. Isn't that the journalist man? "Finally," her voice echoed further away "Took fucking forever" Her heels stopped sharply as she now entered the dining area. Terry saw the blonde with blue eyes clearly. It wasn't an illusion. It was her; it makes sense. "Well, well, well," She said smugly, folding her arms "Long time no see, Diaz" Oh, how her saying her surname filled her with rage. Boiling, bubbling rage. Terry pulled her body forward thinking she could just break free from the ropes and hit her dead straight in the face. But it only shuffled the chair. "Ah, ah, ah!" She tested, walking over to her, turning her chair, and lifting her chin "Now Diaz, we don't want to do anything dumb and get little Jacoby and Amanda in trouble, now do we?" Terry froze to those names. Bailey smiled. "humph" She then stood tall "Once your friends here wake up, we will be explaining what's going to happen" Bailey then pulled down her gag- "What did you do to them!? Where are they!??" She shouted "Terry, calm down Hun. They are safe. Currently in each bedroom sleeping away, after all" She looked at Jason and smiled "We need them to be healthy for the wedding" "Wedding?" "You know, our wedding? I mean, you did see the invitation. It's no lie, Diaz" she said abruptly. Bailey then snapped her fingers at Jason as he jumped at the faint sound. He then dug his hand into his back pocket and lifted out a small navy box. "Do you know what this is?" She said taking it. Terry didn't say anything but locked her eyes on the box. She knew exactly what it was. She couldn't believe they were going this far. Bailey then opened it to such a beautiful, jeweled ring. Terry wasn't going to lie. It was stunning, but it was in such wrong hands.

"Little Jacoby will be sliding this bad boy right on my finger," she said, flexing her hand. "I know Jacob, he wouldn't dare to!" Jason then laughed behind Bailey grimly. "Oh yeah? Tell that to them. They've already agreed to this" Jacob and Amanda agreeing to this whole plan? It just doesn't make sense. They would never. Terry knew there was something behind this, blackmail possibly. Terry then said "But they are married. It can't be legal. It won't work you fucking idiots!" "Jason, show this bitch the papers," Bailey said. Jason then took out a folded piece of paper out of his jeans, again, almost like he had everything in there. He liked to have important things close to him so that he knows where it is. He unfolded it, almost shoving it into Terry's face. She looked at him, that lair who stepped foot in the precinct, and her eyes traced over the neat writing. The structure is so formal. The lower she got her heart began beating faster and her eyes got wider. Divorce papers, signed by those recognizable signatures. But surely it wasn't fully consented just yet? Didn't it need to be cleared by a lawyer? Confirmed? "Signed by little Santiago and Peralta" Jason sniggered, snatching it away. "I should have killed you when I had the chance!" Terry almost spats at Bailey. "Yeah," she leaned down "You should've"

A manda finally felt comfy, warm, and safe. Her hands grazed over a soft sheet under a pillow as she inhaled through her nose, well, partly. She still felt wick like a horrible rainy day as her nose was blocked. But she finally felt some comfort. She opened her eyes slowly, yawning. Mind not so awake yet. She turned her body onto her back and rubbed her eyes. Forgetting what happened, where she was, or what was around her. She just felt like it was home, right in her bed, no Bailey and no Jason. Safe. She pushed her weak body up and plucked open both eyes, half open due to her tiredness. Her eyes looked around the room, not her room, but someone's. But her mind didn't click, it was delayed by the fact everything was still certainly happening. Amanda stretched her arms, also feeling icky with sweat. She was incredibly warm. She realized she was still in her tactical gear. Cargo trousers and her NYPD sweatshirt. She felt like a living fire. It only took ten seconds later when her eyes opened wide in shock, remembering where she was, who she was with, and everything that was happening. It made her jump, scrambling out of bed. But the minute Amanda placed her foot onto the floor, her legs decided to switch off. She was weaker now. The sickness was winning the battle, and she needed that antidote. Amanda drooled over it. She fell to her knees, groaning at the pain and the unbearable throbbing throat. This was worse than any other flu. It felt like someone taking a cat's claws to her esophagus and scratching at any sudden coughs or swallowing. Her legs felt like her feet were clamped to heavy weights and her mouth was dryer sandpaper. Amanda was in the dying need of fresh, iced water. She put one knee up and placed her hand on top. Giving all her strength to push herself up. Finally, she was on two feet. It was a struggle and was hard to focus on her blurred vision. But she adjusted. Amanda needed to see Jacob. Where was he? Wait! The squad. She was in the beehouse, they had to be here. They should be. She then went over to the door and turned the knob. It was locked.

"No," she said to herself, shaking the door again "No!" She gripped it harder. Amanda gave up and kicked the door with her foot in a childish act. She was surprised by the fact that she had the strength for that. Amanda turned herself and looked around the room. Her eyes set upon a window. She then went over to it in a slight rush. She pulled up, as hard as she could but the latch was locked. Everything was locked. Jason and Bailey, another point to them on the scoreboard. Just then Amanda heard the door opening, as the door handle squeaked to its movement. She turned her body round to see Jason at the door, holding a glass of water. He knew exactly what she was doing. "Princess, we've locked everything. You're not going anywhere" he said so calming. Princess? Amanda hated that nickname. She hated anything that came out of his putrid mouth. "Jacob" She replied bluntly "Where is he?" "In a room, sleeping away. Getting ready for the big night" he said, now walking closer to her. "Big night? You mean-" "Yes, Amanda. We are getting married tonight. The longer we wait. The harder it is to keep your friends trying to be the heroes," He then stopped right at her and stretched out his arm with the glass in his hand "Here" Amanda looked at the water. It looked so much better than a Thanksgiving meal. It looked so fresh and cold as there was cold condensation dripping on the outside. It seemed too similar and relevant to a fresh Coca-Cola bottle in a TV advert. Amanda licked her parched lips and grabbed the glass, guzzling the pure, breath-taking water that slid down her blazing throat. She didn't care that it hurt. She didn't care at all. "Woah, slow down" He laughed taking the glass "You'll make yourself throw up" Amanda wiped her mouth with her free sleeve and looked down. "Thanks..." She said meekly "Yeah, okay," he said, trying to stay in character. He then went to the door and held the handle "If you need more, just say-." He stopped himself. He had to stay strict ... mean. "You'll wait till I come back" Jason then was about to close the door to a shut but stopped at Amanda calling out. "Wait" She rushed to the door and Jason looked back at her. "What?" he replied resentfully Amanda bit her lip. She needed to have an excuse to get out of that room and see where everyone was. Where Jacob was. She stuttered. "Bathroom!" She shouted, then cleared her throat "Bathroom... I need to go to the bathroom..." she said sheepishly. Jason glared at her for a while, like he knew something was up. Amanda began to sweat more. It was a tense moment. Jason sighed and pinched his eyes in disparity. "Alright. Five minutes, that's it! I can't make my own decisions" He looked behind him "Bailey wouldn't be pleased..." Jason then opened the door wider "Go" Amanda bowed her head and took one step but was stopped by Jason grabbing her sweatshirt "I mean it. Five minutes" He finally let go. Amanda nodded again and went to one of the bathrooms down the hall, shutting the door and pushing her back against the door. She sighed in relief. She felt safe with a lock on the door. The real reason why she needed out of that room, was to find something to defend herself. Attack. A weapon.

Surely there was something in the bathroom that could help. Amanda began to rummage through the cupboards, drawers, and units. Nothing, all she came across were hairbrushes, toothbrushes, bubbles, hair gel, deodorants, and even condoms. She didn't even want to think about that. But strangely there was a tin in one of the drawers. Odd for something to be there. But it doesn't hurt anyone to look. Hopefully nothing like what she found before... She discreetly took off the lid and saw what was inside. A sewing kit. Needles, threads, buttons, and, oh yes. Bing pot. Scissors. She no longer wants to question why there was a sewing kit in the bathroom. But thank God for it. Amanda then placed it into one of her pouches in her navy cargo jeans and fixed everything in the bathroom. She took one deep breath and walked out of the bathroom. But was struck by Jason standing right at the door. It scared the hell out of her. "J-Jason! Hehe... what up bro?" He looked down at her like she was nothing to him. A small weak bug. Sick bug. He then grabbed her by the throat. "What were you doing in there!?" Amanda pulled at his hand. His grip wasn't tight, it was enough to still talk. "Nothing! I just wanted to freshen up" she said in fear. But this was her opportunity. She secretly reached for her pouch at her leg but was struggling. "Don't lie to me, Ames... What were you doing? I heard you!" His grip tightened and Amanda's mind began to worry. She was desperately trying to reach into her pocket. Fumbling her hand secretly "Answered me!" he shook. Amanda pulled her hand down further, pulling and pulling. Jason's grip got tighter. Her fingers kept grazing the tip of the handles. But she couldn't reach it. If she lifted her leg, it would make it noticeable. "I SAID ANSWER ME!" Finally... She wrapped her hand over the full metallic scissors. "Oh nothing..." she laughed "maybe getting-THIS!" Just then she stabbed him right in the shoulder, making him let go of her throat and groan. Grabbing at his shoulder. Amanda didn't dare to leave it in his skin, she took one jab and straight out. Jason bent over groaning. Amanda froze at what she had done, but her mind suddenly screamed. RUN! RUN! And she did, she ran down the hall, right into the lounge area where Bailey and Shea sat on the seats, watching the flickering orange fireplace dance. And of course, they spotted her. Eyes wide. "Amanda Santiago," Shea sat up "What a pleasant surprise! It seems you're lost...?" Amanda's heart was racing. She was panting. She then looked down at the dining table and saw Terry, weakly looking down while the rest were out cold and tied up. Outside it was becoming dusk. "Terry! "Amanda called out and ran to her. Terry snapped her head up and saw a very, pale, sick-looking Amanda running towards her. "Amanda!?" Suddenly, just as Amanda thought she could sprint into the lounge area and try to jump over a sofa past Bailey and get to Terry. She thought wrong. Amanda felt her leg being snagged and fell harshly on her chest on the couch, Dropping the scissors in her hand and flying and gliding to Terry, as she wasn't as far away from her. Terry's chair was turned away from the table, so she was able to see them accidentally slide to her and hide under her heeled boot. "So, you think I am playing games now, huh!?" She said turning Amanda around on her back. She then pulled out her knife that always sat on the side of her belt and directly placed it on Amanda's old scar. The same place where she was attacked in the school shooting. "Let's play then" Bailey sinisterly smiled and dug right into her flesh. "I'll be the Doctor!" She said through her gritted teeth. Digging it in harder. "And you'll be the patient!" Amanda screamed in pain, howled, and kicked her legs. Her weak, shaking legs. In the other room, Jacob heard a scream. Amanda's scream. He just woke 3 minutes ago, hearing strange commotion, but wasn't fully functioning. Now he was. He was more awake now hearing her screams. He ran out of bed, scrambling, weak, falling to his knees but shooting back up. He crashed his body into the door and screamed her name. "Amanda!" He slammed himself again "AMES!" But Amanda couldn't hear him. Her screaming and moaning were loud. Her eyes were shut and hands over Baileys. She desperately tried to pull it out. She tried so hard, but she was stronger. "Tay!" Jason suddenly shouted from behind. She flicked her head and looked at him. "Let go of her!" He threatened "As much as she fucking deserves it! I need her alive!" "A little stab won't do harm. Isn't that right shea?" "Seems fine to me" He replied smugly. "It will make a good Twitter video" Amanda then pulled the sharp blade out of her and Bailey looked down. She didn't complain about the fact Amanda handled her precious knife, instead, she smiled. "Looks like your little Prince charming saved the day" She then pulled Amanda up who was holding her pouring wound. She could feel her warm blood collect on her hand and soak her sweatshirt. Amanda was shaking like mad and was in impeccable pain. She was so weak that she was ready to faint. She wanted everything to end. She wanted to be out. Amanda wanted to be free. Jason then walked over, also holding the side of his shoulder, and looked at Bailey with a glare. She smiled, pushing Amanda to him as he caught her in time. "It's quite pathetic Jason, the fact that little weak worm defeated you. Is quite embarrassing" She stepped closer "If I were you... I would keep a closer eye on this sneaky one. I know what she is capable of. Now take her and get her ready. I'm not waiting anymore." She then turned to Terry and the rest of the squad who seemed to be waking up "This wedding is happening now."

Chapter 15: A Puppet

Amanda fell into Jason's arms. Not wanting to, but she was that weak, so beat down, that she needed to be held. She needed someone else to hold her up like a puppet. That's what she felt like. A puppet with strings. In control by the insane, playing to their entertainment as they clap their hands and laugh ruthlessly. That's exactly how it felt. She couldn't do anything outside of their command. After all, they do hold something they need. The antidote. Amanda grew weaker and weaker, almost sinking and melting away in Jason's hold. Her eyes betrayed her, feeling heavy and wanting to close so badly. How Amanda would love a long, rejuvenating sleep. Forgetting everything. Being back to when things were normal. Only a genie can grant that wish now. Amanda lost hope. She dropped it, no longer wanting to hold onto it. "This wedding is happening now!" Amanda heard Bailey shout "I'm no longer waiting around..." She wanted to react. But couldn't. All her mind was fixed on was her wound. She could feel her own blood soak into her sweatshirt. Her hand was layered with it. It was placed right over it, held on tightly to stop the flow. But obviously, it wasn't working. "Get her out of my sight. Get her patched up or something. Just make sure she is still alive." Bailey said, while cleaning her knife on the side of her black jeans and sliding it back into her belt. "I'll sort out the other one" Jason nodded his head, disappointed almost. He felt ashamed being attacked by a puny little cop. He looked down at Amanda who seemed to be not a part of the world. He rolled his eyes, pulled her off his chest, no longer holding her, and grabbed Amanda by her wrists. He led her back down the hall as she stammered behind. Jason then took her into the previous room and let go, slamming the door and pushing her forwards, deeper into the bedroom. Amanda stood in the middle of the room, holding her shoulder, swaying. Although her eyes glared at Jason who walked around her and was now stroking his chin in thought, pacing backwards and forwards. "I should've left you in here!" He then snapped "See what happens when you make stupid mistakes!!?" He began to walk to her. "I trusted you!!!" His eyes locked onto hers. But Amanda kept her glare. Just then, Jason's mood changed like a flick of a switch. He stood tall and inhaled deeply through his nose. Made his two hands into a prayer symbol, put it by his lips, and heavily exhaled. "I trusted you..." He said, now ever so calming "But instead, Princess, you disobeyed my rules" He then said, grabbing her chin and lifting her head softly. Amanda stared into his eyes. It was like she could see the insanity swim in those blue eyes. It sent chills down her spine. He could just snap in any moment and God knows what he could do. She then looked at his shoulder. It was also seeping with blood through his T-shirt. "But I guess you got what you deserved" he then spoke, looking at Amanda's hand placed on her shoulder. "See what happens when we try to play the hero?" He then took her hand, but Amanda snatched it back. Afraid like a lost puppy. But he smiled affectionately, yet so insanely at the same time. "I'm trying to help, princess" "Don't call me princess" Amanda replied bitterly "Oh, Amanda. You are my princess though. Just imagine! Me, you, and our little child. Out of New York, somewhere with clear skies and blue beaches. No one to bother us and you are being treated like royalty. That's why you are my princess, Amanda" "You're crazy! You are both crazy! You think you can get away with this!?" Amanda shrieked. The thought of his dream was frightening. She didn't want to be with him. No. She wanted to see Jacob. She is with Jacob, and they will always be together.

"Accept it, Ames. You're not going to go anywhere. You've lost. Game over. It's the End for you and Jacob. We've already won" He then took her by the side of her arms and pushed her down gently onto the bed. Amanda looked down, not daring to make eye contact. "I thought you were different..." She spoke. Jason scoffed "What's that supposed to mean?" "I thought at one point you would finally open your eyes. See the good" Amanda looked up to him "You're different from Bailey. I know you are" Jason clamped his jaw and walked over to one of the units with drawers in the room. He pulled out his bag, where he must have placed it, and walked back to Amanda. "Bailey is different" He began "She's not a bad person, Amanda. Neither am I" He then pulled out scissors "We've just experienced some things" He then began to cut the collar of her sweatshirt, revealing her wound. "Hit some bumps, that's all" Jason then pulled out a white bottle, flipped the cap open, and squirted it into a white cloth. He seems to have everything in that bag. Prepared. I wonder what else... Just suddenly, he placed it on her gash, making Amanda inhale through her teeth in pain. It jabbed her like a thorn, stung like a wasp, and hurt like hell. Amanda groaned, grabbing the bedsheets in anticipation. Making her knuckles go white. But Jason continues. "I've made mistakes, so has Bailey. But that doesn't make us evil, Amanda. It doesn't justify who we are-" "It does!" Amanda said through her pain. "No, Princess. It doesn't. I can make bad choices and I can make good" He then took a bandage and unrolled it "What I'm doing now, is a good choice. Me marrying you, is a good choice. As for Bailey?" he laughed, then placing it on Amanda's shoulder. "Sure, she is different. But whatever you see in me?" he finally looked at her. "Is false" Amanda began to cry. Was this really it? Jason took her face again gently. "This is our future"

Jacob shook at the door handle as best as he could, slamming his body and everything. He kept calling Amanda's name. Over and over. Her screams stopped a while ago, but he still pined to be out there. He needed to see her. "Amanda!" He kicked the door once again "Hold on, Ames! Just hold on!" But his body became heavier. Jacob was now panting, mind going slightly fuzzy. Those pills. Those pills are absolute hell. He's never felt this way before. Jacob decided to give up, shaking with fear for Amanda. Even the squad. He never saw them coming in. That's all he wanted was to see his wife and friends. All was going wrong. They were cops! Cops are being beaten by three insane people with no anguish. No heart. No soul. That's the way he saw them. Jacob flopped onto the previous bed he was sleeping in. He felt icky. Glazed with sweat. He was too warm still in his tactical gear. He lay on his back, hands covering his face, and sighed. What to do? "Hey Jacoby" A voice called out to him. Jacob sat up in fright and saw Amanda standing at the door, smiling, almost grinning. She looked smug. Taller as well. "Oh! Thank God you're okay!" He ran to her, wrapping his arms around her body. Jacob then cupped her face "What happened to you? Are you hurt?" "Me? No, no. No one can hurt me Jacoby" she replied.

But something was off about her. She seemed too proud of something and too complacent. Not to mention she never called him Jacoby. Jacob looked into her brown loving eyes, frowning, cupping her face. "Amanda?" he said softly. "She's fine..." Amanda spoke. Or so Jacob thought. Amanda's hair became blonde and her eyes switched blue. It was all an illusion. His mind was going mad. Jacob jumped in fright, snatched his hands off her face, and backed away. Shocked and confused. "Let's just say, she had to learn her mistakes" Bailey then said, now so clear it was her. "You-You're not Amanda" Jacob stuttered. Now covering his forehead "You're not Amanda- I saw Amanda-I-" "Ahh..." Bailey smiled now walking in and closing the door "Illusions? Seeing things now, Jacob?" Jacob looked up now, still so very confused. What was going on with him? He saw his wife. He was sure! But Bailey scoffed and folded her arms. "Seems like someone jumped to stage 4" She then walked over and took his face "The last stage" Jacob ripped his face away from her and stood tall. Trying to seem stronger than what he was feeling. "And what!? What's going to happen?" He shouted in her face. So much rage now. "You're not long away from now suffering from terrible headaches, illusions, and even death, Jacob." she said in such a monotone voice "I didn't expect you to jump this fast into this stage. But I guess it's a good time to get the show going" "Death!? What do you mean!!?" Bailey laughed shortly. "Your body decides to shut down. Gives up and waves the white flag" Jacob was now sweating with fear. This cannot be happening. This couldn't happen. Suddenly he winced, groaning and grabbing his head. Falling onto his knees. His head pounded. Banging and felt horrible. It felt like someone pushing the side of his head inwards or even drilling something into his brain. The pain was unbearable. So sore that he even wanted to pull out his hair "GAHHH!" He groaned "Make it stop! Make it stop! Agha!" Bailey then crouched down and smiled down at him. Almost like she was enjoying his pain. "It will stop after you say these two words, Jacoby." She then leaned in closer and hissed "I do"

Shea stood in front of the dining table, watching everyone groan in agony, waking up slowly. He was grinning. His arms were folded but most importantly, his eyes were locked on Ashley. His heart softly pounded as her eyes fluttered open, and her hands became calamander. Shea was technically fan Girling over her. Crazy, right? Terry looked at Shea drilling his eyes into her. It created something she doesn't always like to feel. An emotion. Jealousy was cooking up inside her. Ashley was her ditzy love. She was annoying at times, but she is hers. It was unusual of course. Almost like Shea knew her as his eyes seemed to sparkle with joy. Terry then looked over and called out Ashley's name as she saw her move "Ashley!?" She called out but in reply she sighed and groaned, watching her hair graze across her face. "Ashley! It's me!" "Beyonce...?" She croaked, still eyes closed. She felt awful. "Yes, Ashley. Beyonce" Terry said sarcastically, tied in with an eye roll "It's me, you goof. Terry?"

Ashley then finally opened her eyes to meet with Terry. Terry's eyes softened to her look, and she smiled. It's a very rare thing to make Diaz do. "No offense," She cleared her throat "Beyonce would be way better waking up to" "Ashley... I-I-" Shea stuttered, nervous about what to say. She then turned her head to him and looked up and down. Almost with disgust. Ashley didn't even think twice about why she was tied up. "And who are you?" She asked, looking at Shea up and down. Shea scoffed and nervously rubbed the back of his neck. He was even blushing. Terry's emotion grew. "It's Shea" He spoke, standing highly "I know you of your socials Twitter and all that cool stuff..." Ashley squinted her eyes, observing the man who was standing in front. Green eyes, brunette hair... Broad body. He looked familiar. Ashley's mind finally clicked. Her eyes widened with shock. "Omg, shea? As in Shea Robinson!?" she scoffed in laughter "Damn, son. Puberty hit you like a bus!" "YOU KNOW ME!!? I- I mean" Shea cleared his throat and lowered his voice. Trying to hide his excitement "You know me? How come?" "Dude, I've literally been searching for you to ask where you got your shoes from when you totally robbed me" "Oh them? Their Balenciaga's, nothing much" He shrugged "You can get them around like £720 pound really. Good quality! But that's beside the point-" "Is that what the hell is going on!!?" Terry interrupted. "Calm down gurl, just catch up with this goon" She gestured her head to Shea "Which, by the way. By any chance did you steal one of my Ashley hoodies?" She turned back round to him. Shea's heart slightly fluttered again. He couldn't believe it. He was talking to Ashley! His love! His mind was swimming in loving thoughts. But he had to stay focused. "First of all, I'm no goon, and yes, it's not my fault they were out of stock. But like, 'A' has been washed off, so it is now "Gin knows best", Which, quite frankly, still works well. But how about you cut me a deal, give me one for half price" Ashley sucked in her teeth in thought and stalled for a bit. Only to tease him. "Yedaiah, no. I'm a more forward person. But half price isn't going to cut it. Just like you are stealing my hoodie. Oh, damn, Ashley!" Shea knitted his eyebrows and was rather shocked at her comment. At the same time, Terry kicked the scissors, that were previously under her boot, near her hands that were tied behind the chair. Terry tried to pull her body slightly down by not making it noticeable. But it was a struggle. Her fingers kept grazing the handle, brushing against her skin. It hurt to stretch her arms against her length as they sat on the floor. "Did you just oh damn yourself?" Shea spoke "Someone had to" Ashley pouted. Shea rolled his eyes and continued. "Whatever. Plus, I didn't steal, I borrowed it for like... maybe... for life ... but that's not the point, Linette. The point is that you are finally here, with me!" After those words and watching them two talk away. Terry finally snapped, stopping at what she was doing, and glared. Her emotion escaped like a frantic cadged animal. "You are better back the fuck off, dipshit!" Terry threatened, pulling her body forwards. "Ooh Yeah. Did I forget to mention I'm gay?" Ashley giggled, winking at Terry.

But Shea didn't react. Instead, he kept it inside. It hurt a little. But it still didn't stop him from having her. Not at all. Shea had his plan for what he was going to do and held onto it tight. He folded his arms and leaned all his weight to one leg. "That doesn't surprise me actually" he conveyed "And Terry, I'm not here to steal Ashley and take her by the arm and run to the sunset. I'm here to be friends with her. So, calm your flat ass" "Shea, you're meant to greet our guests with kindness" It was Bailey who spoke, walking towards the dining area where all the squad sat in chairs. She spoke softly but in an obvious sarcastic way. It was Bailey's signature thing. "I am treating them with respect, but it doesn't look like they want to respect me." Shea said, "Isn't that right, Terry?" She scowled at him, wanting to spit in his face so badly. But she remained put. Terry knew the time when it was right. Instead, she continued to try to reach her wants. Those scissors are the only way to save everyone. "Good afternoon, squad" Bailey raised her voice in a welcome "Glad to see your faces again" "I could say the same for you, but I prefer not to lie" Holt finally spoke. Not making eye contact. "Ahh, captain. Your humor gets me all the time-" "Jacob!?" Charles intervened, constantly pulling at the ropes around his chest. "Where is he!?" Bailey glanced at Shea and so did he. They both smiled synchronously. She then smiled, clearly satisfied with herself. "Little Jacoby is fine. As for Santiago? She will be okay" Bailey then clapped her hands together "Now! To the point. As you would already know, I'm marrying Jacob" She paused, looking at the shocked blank faces "I know, don't congratulate me all at once. But you guys are very lucky to be here to witness this very special day-" Suddenly Scully cut her halfway "Will there be cake?" Bailey's face dropped and confusingly looked at him. Out of all the things he had to say, was that. "No... there isn't" "YOU MONSTER! HOW COULD YOU DO THIS!?" He yelled back "We all know it's illegal not to have a cake at a wedding!" Hitchcock responds. "Ow, come on man. That's what you ask!?" Terry questioned. Shuffling in his seat. "Enough!" The curly blonde shouted "There is no fucking cake, this isn't like any other wedding! You all are going to watch and accept this is happening. Try to make a move? Your friends will die of their own sickness! I hold their only escape" she pulled out the antidote "And if any of you want to ruin this night?" Bailey laughed maniacally "It's the last of you, and your little friends" She walked away, stomping her heels that made a clicking sound surface around the house. But suddenly, a low dropping shallow sound growled outside. A small sound of millions of raindrops tapping on the glass appeared. Darkness was now in the sky. Thunder and rain collided together outside, sounding like banging drums. What a perfect scenography. But Bailey loved that. It made her feel like she was finally winning. Finally stronger. She opened the front door, no hesitation on walking outside into the howling rain, and made her way to the car. She ripped open the trunk to reveal to me a red dress and a jet-black, slick suit. Not belonging to her obviously. But to Jacob and Amanda. She grinned. Taking the clothing and pulling out a black case. She flicked the lid open, showing inside a black foam. But it had two molded shapes. Just the right size for the antidote to smoothly slide right in. That's what the case's purpose was for. They were ready for this day.

Bailey always planned. She was like that as a kid. She liked to be ahead and organized. She was smart, but pretty. So, everyone stereotyped her to be the popular dumb blonde. They were wrong. Just like how Jacob was wrong to leave her all alone. Abandon her. No longer will that happen. She slid the small glass capsule of liquid into the mound and walked back to the beach house. It was warmer in there.

The fireplace heated the house up and painted the white walls orange. It was a relaxing look. Bailey made her way to the room Amanda and Jason were in, not wanting to knock. She opened it to Amanda sitting on the bed, groaning while Jason patched her up. "Five minutes" She threw the red dress "Out here and ready" Bailey shut the door once again and walked into Jacobs. He was a mess. Still weirdly attractive to Bailey's view. But he looked pale. On the edge of death... Which they both were. He lay curled up on the bed, shivering. "Hey Jacoby," she said innocently He looked up, squinting his eyes like he was seeing someone else. "And no. It's not Amanda. It's your fiancée." she then held up his suit "Now, put this on. Our day awaits"

20 minutes later Amanda pulled on her red dress. Her bold red dress. She was finally alone in the room after Jason patched her up and demanded change. She had no choice. Amanda looked at herself in the mirror. It was like she was looking at a stranger. Her eyes were dull, and her face was not the natural color. Her hair remained up in a ponytail. She didn't want this to happen. Where was Jacob? Was he okay? What about the squad? How are they doing? Her mind was drowning. Anxiety began to climb, and tears began to fall. Here she was. Failing her friends. Letting them down. And their baby. What would happen to it? Amanda stroked her stomach, almost like she could feel her little baby. She wanted it to be safe. "I won't let him hurt you..." She whispered to herself as tears ran down her cheeks. But a knock appeared on the door, making her swing round and see who it was. To no surprise. It was Bailey. "Hello Santiago," she said at the door. Amanda turned her back to her, wiped her tears away with her hand, and sniffed "What do you want now, huh? Drug me again? Maybe pop in another pill?" "No" she walked towards her and zipped up her red dress in the back "I'm here to help you" She then placed her hands on Amanda's shoulders. Looking into the mirror she was standing in "After

all. We will be family" Those words slid down Amanda's spine and made her shiver in fear. Family. That's one thing she never thought of hearing from her. She kept her head down. "Aww... Little Amanda" She pulled her head back up to meet Bailey's reflection "Don't look so dull" She then delicately pulled out her ponytail, making Amanda's hair now sit on her shoulders with her natural curl "Don't look so upset, after all. It is our wedding" Amanda said nothing but looked at the body who stood in front with a red dress on. That was really her, huh? She was really living in that body. Amanda's eyes began to deceive her. She didn't want to be there. She hated herself for letting this happen. How did she let this happen? How? She doesn't know. But this was it. The end. She was sick, weak, and in desperate need of that antidote. It sounded better than freshwater or a nicely cooked meal. Come to think of it. She was starving. But that antidote was circling in her mind. She needed that. Earlier when Jason left the room, she began to see her Mom and Dad. Just standing in the corner, saying how proud they were of her. But they disappeared. Amanda didn't know where, but they weren't real. She was seeing things. "Now, they are outside waiting on us. Everyone is there to watch. I think we are ready. Don't you?" Bailey spoke, fixing her hair. Amanda inhaled deeply and took one last look at herself. Here it goes. The final game. "I'm ready..."

Chapter 16: Burning Soul

Terry was secretly in distress. She still tried ever so hard to grab those scissors behind her on the floor. She continuously stretched out her hand to grab them. But her fingers just grazed over the handles every time, or she accidentally moved them by an inch. It wasn't easy. Ahead, shea and Jason were moving furniture in the living area. Clearly getting that area moved for the "wedding". The fireplace was lit, and outside was now a dark sheet of black. Rain drummed outside and to no surprise, thunder roared and echoed. The moment was unsettling for the squad. They were all tied. Weakly watching their friends getting roped into this madness. There was nothing for them to do. Their best detectives' and friends' lives were at major risk. They were at deaths door. Bailey discussed about their sickness. It broke them all. Scared them. Haunted them. Awoke a sinister feeling of fear in them. What can they do? They are cops! They had to think of something, right? "We can't let this happen" Charles spoke from the other side of the table "Jacob and Amanda are meant to be forever married!" "Never mind those circumstances, they are both in great danger." Holt then awoke his voice, looking at the two men in the living room "Whatever they gave them, is seriously damaging their bodies" "Ugh! You guys are cops" Ashley then vexed "Terry. You got muscles on muscles; can't you break those ropes?" Terry exhaled through his nose and tightened his muscles, pulling up as the vein on his head bulged out. Terry then sighed. "It's useless, man. Terry can't do it" Everyone at the table fell silent.

More in thought of Jacob and Amanda. They have been through so much. Holt then spoke. "I should've never let them go to that place. Especially Amanda" "Captain, none of this is your fault. No one knew this was going to happen. Sometimes we can't control the controllable" Ashley worded, not sarcastically for once. Holt sat on his seat quite perplexed the conversation was still struggling. Her mind was too focused on that shiny object on the floor. She almost had it. She could feel it. "Check up on those cops up there" She heard shea say to Jason. It sent a panic shock through her body. What if they found it? "Come on..." Terry mumbled to herself as she was trying to pick up the scissors, watching shea walk up. "Come on!" Her fingers kept grazing over it. Her heart was thumping, and arms began to ache. She almost had it. Fear pulsed through her like a circuit. Jason then looked at Terry's expressions. He knew something was up. "Hey?" He quickened his walk "What the hell are you doing?" Terry gave no answer but instead stared at him blankly. She didn't on Ashley's speech. For her to say something like that, was rare. "You know, for you Ashley, that was actually a very smart thing to quote" "I'm Ashley Linette. I'm full of many surprises" she replied smugly, back to her usual self. On the other side, Terry, not really connected to want to say anything at all "You got a mouth, don't you?" the blue-eyed man threatened. "Obviously" Terry replied with a tone. "Then answer me!" Terry stalled for a second and inhaled. "Nothing" She smiled, trying not to look as inconspicuous "Nothing at all."

Jason didn't buy it. No, not at all. Instead, he leaned in close, eyeing her up and down like she was praying. Something was not right. But Terry kept her emotions straight. Her face was so emotionless. The flickering orange glow from the fire cast shadows on her face. "Hiding something?" Jason smiled. But Terry said nothing. In response, he got a stone-cold look tied in with silence, well, partly silence as the rain slapped against the windows. He then stood tall, put his hands around his back and slowly paced around Terry. Her chair wasn't tucked into the table like the others. She slightly was placed away from it. Her chair faced away from the table and faced the fireplace in the living room. Jason then stopped behind her back and looked down at her tied hands. Nothing. He then looked at the floor. Nothing. "Hohm" He then came back round to her face "I wouldn't want to be doing anything stupid" Jason's eyes then wandered around, looking at the squad. "Wouldn't want to ruin the show, now do we?" he continued. "You guys will sit here, not even a peep, and watch Amanda become mine" "They wouldn't. She loves Jacob!" Charles pitched in "You're right" He smiled devilishly "She does love Jacob. But what will she take more? The only stop to her sickness. Or death?" Everyone was dead silent. What could they say to that? There was nothing. Nothing to say. Nothing to do. "I rest my case..." He dipped his tone, walking away and back into the living room. They really were serious about this. Candles were lit on tall metal stands, half the size of Jason. There were three of them. One set is on the left side of the fireplace and another set is on the right. Jason found them, somewhere in the house. There was a gap in the middle, dead center of the lounge area and fireplace. That, that right there, was where the ceremony was happening. But what really caught everyone's eye was a briefcase sitting on a small square table, just enough to fit coffee mugs, placed to a side. That briefcase held those tasty, succulent, liquid gold, antidotes. Just two small glass tubes topped with a small black cap. Suddenly Coughing came echoing down the hall. Jacob stumbled round the corner. Bent over coughing. It sounded crooked. He looked awful. Jacob looked worse, perhaps the definition of pain. But that wasn't the worst thing. He was genuinely wearing a suit. His old wedding suits. The real slick black suit at their wedding. Jacob and Amanda's. Bailey really was prepared. It was almost too scary. "Ahh! There he is the lucky man!" Jason said in glee, winding his arms almost like he was going in for a hug. "You look well. Sharp! Well..." He then looked at Jacob's face "Almost well" "Jacob!" Terry yelled, along with the squad who began to chant his name. But he seemed so delayed. It took him a while to hear the calls to his name. "Guys?" he squinted his eyes. His vision was forbidding him to see far. His headache lowered but still stuck around. Everything hurt. Luckily, he could still stand though. Still move "Don't listen to them, they will be sorted" Jason grabbed his face ruthlessly "This is our night. This is your only chance to finally feel yourself! The real Jacob. The healthy man" He smiled. Jason then fixed his bow tie. "Don't you want that, Jacob?"

"I want you to let them go..."Jacob said with a stern voice. " Take me. Bailey can have me. But leave my friends and Amanda out of it" "Oh Jacob" He laughed shortly "Always so... What's the word?" He teased "Selfless. So Selfless. The hero among the squad. The guy everyone loves! I hate to break it to you, but..." Jason leaned in closer "That's not going to happen. I need her, Jacob. I need Amanda. I need a family. A purpose in my life" Jacob said nothing. He was being beat down. He felt so small now, so ashamed. Some cop he was. He really couldn't do a thing, huh? He was really that weak? That broke down and belittled. Yeah, he was. It was just like that. Jason then walked away from him, going to go to whatever. But Jacob spoke. He said something that made him freeze. "Do you really think she would be proud of you?" Jacob almost said in a whisper. Jason stopped and turned round slowly "What did you say?" "You heard me. You heard every word" He began to walk to him "How would she feel?" Jacob knew his weak spot. His mother. See, he already knew about their mom in high school when he was friends with Bailey. He was there the day she broke down to him about her. He knows the whole story. Now? Now it was his weapon. "It doesn't matter what she thinks!" He said, so outraged. Throwing his hand "She will love me no matter what!" "Is that what you think?" Jacob scoffed "You really are delusional" Jason was so outraged, he was breathing like he was out of breath. Standing speechless. But his mood switched. He stood tall, ran his hands through his hair and inhaled deeply through his nose. "The wedding is about to begin. Unless you would like to die? Step aside now. If you want to live? Take this" He slapped a ring in his hand "And say i do" Jacob looked at the brief case sitting on a small square coffee table, and sighed. Jacob needed that, especially Amanda. He looked down at the ring in his hand, observing every crystal. This was insane. Too crazy to be real. It almost felt like a story. Jacob looked up. Not saying anything but nodded. This was it.

"Ready..." Amanda said. Not happy about it at all. Bailey, behind her, smiled and hummed. Stroking her hair. It was bizarre to see her like this. Every touch sent chills down Amanda's back. "You and I, are now going to become sisters." she said in her ear "Best we start fresh...don't you think? " Amanda couldn't help but to cry. Sisters. Never has she thought the day. That's a nightmare. An utter nightmare. But Amanda jumped out of her daze as Bailey's finger wiped away one of Amanda's scrolling tears. "Try to lose the crying, It makes you look.... Well, let's just say, ugly." She smiled fakery "Let's get going" She gave her flowers to hold "Your groom awaits" Amanda took one last look at her reflection before she was directed away. The door opened and the sound to drumming rain was louder. Amanda couldn't help but to feel faint. Not only due to her sickness, but out of utter fear.

She came round a corner to meet her friends all now gagged up at the dinner table. All their brows were knitted together in fear. Terry's face glowed the most under the orange flame. "GUYS-" she screamed but was stopped by Baileys, hurtful grip around her shoulder and was pushed towards Jason. He stood in the middle, among candles sitting on long metal stands. His face was smiling with joy- Jacob! Jacob stood right next to him. Amanda's heart stopped. Not fear this time, but in glee. He was okay! "Jacob..." She said meekly, spreading her arms, ready to hug him. But Jason stepped in front and grabbed her chin gently. "You look beautiful, princess" He smiled affectionately down at her. Amanda glared up with fearful eyes. "Come, join me." He took her hands and pulled her in the middle. On the other hand, Bailey walked up to Jacob and placed her hands on his chest. "I've been dreaming this day, Jacoby. This is finally the day. Me, you. Back together. Just like old times!" She then cupped his face "And no one can get in our way" Jacob snatched his face away. All four stood in front of the fireplace. Jacob's back was turned to the antidotes but was facing Bailey. In front of Amanda, stood Jason. But his back was turned away from Jacob, Bailey, and the briefcase. The rest of the squad sat helplessly at the back with gags now. But Terry was already on the move. Little did Jason know. She had the scissors slipped up her leather jacket. Cuddled away. Now she was sawing away. Cutting the small strands of the rope. Holt saw what she was doing and kept an eye out. He remained calm. He now had a plan. "Shea. Do the honors?" Bailey smiled, festering her head to be their official Priest. "Don't expect much. I don't know what the hell to say" Shea stepped forward and cleared his throat. "Uh... We are all gathered here today, to... Um..." He stuttered "Witness this special day of these four lucky people" Jason then took Amanda's hands. Her cold hands and smiled at her. "Bailey, would you like to go first?" Shea continued Bailey nodded and looked back at Jacob. Her smile was so grim that it turned Jacob's stomach. He took one last glance at Amanda who seemed to be looking at something else. Jacob wanted to tell her one last time how much he loved her. "Eyes front, Jacoby." She snapped "Now... The ring?" Jacob opened his hand. There is sat. All he had to do was slide it onto her finger. That would be it. Then, he can drink that desired liquid. "Do you, Bailey Irvine, take Jacob here to be your beloved husband?" Shea said Bailey's smile stretched more and muffled sounds came from the back, coming from the squad who were disagreeing. "I do" She discreetly slid the ring on his finger. Jacob looked down at it. It was that surreal. It didn't feel real at all.

"And do you, Jacob Peralta, take Bailey to be your wife?" Those words looped in his head. He looked at Bailey. Now looking deep into her blue eyes brought so many memories. High school scars. The time when Bailey was a regular girl. Likable too. "Well?" Bailey asked impatiently. But he didn't respond instantly. He took one last look at his friend's. Especially Charles. Jacob's heart was crumpled. His face was written in sorrow and fear. But Amanda. She looked at him with such daring eyes. Such a look that he has never seen before. It Broke him but he didn't want them to die. "I..." He stalled, looking at the ring "I do." And just like that. He slid it on. Oh, how Bailey's smile stretched more. It was horrifying. Never has he seen her smile so much. But she was now happy. Maybe more than happy. Jacob was hers. All hers. She grabbed his face and kissed it. Caressing his lips. But Jacob didn't act back. No. He didn't dare to kiss the insane blonde back. But she let go, almost gasping in desire, and licked her lips "Here you go Jacoby," She said, now carefully taking out the small tube "You've done well," Jacob snatched it with no hesitation and downed the thing. It was barely anything. But it felt so good sliding down his throat. It tasted sour, but that didn't matter. He was cured. He was free. But he didn't instantly feel different. That's until he could feel something cold rush up his body, through his veins like a burst of ice. Was it working? "Now, Amanda, do you take Jason to be your beloved husband?" Amanda kept eyeing the briefcase. Not daring to look at Jason. She didn't want to say a word. Amanda wanted to find a way out. "Princess..." He heard him speak in a luring tone. But she didn't care. Amanda was eyeing her situation. Just then she looked at Terry. This time, she was nodding. Why was she nodding? Amanda frowned and looked at her closer. Her hands were free. She waved her hand secretly at her to let Amanda know. "Princess!?" Amanda sharply turned her head to meet his gaze. Those blue eyes. But she smiled. Even Jason was slightly confused at that. "Say it" He continued "Say it and it will be all over" Amanda inhaled, still smiling. "I do..." Jason relaxed, about to bring out his hand to receive his ring. He saw it come close to his finger and- "Not fucking think so!" Amanda continued. She punched him right in the crotch and ran for the briefcase. Terry then stood up, cutting loose holts ropes as quickly as possible. Strands began to break piece by piece. She was sweating with fear, trembling. That's all she was focused on was cutting away. Then it broke free.

"Take this and cut everyone else free!" She said in a rush, pulling down his gag. She then ran towards Shea and kicked him in the back of his legs, making him fold to the ground. Amanda on the other hand got her leg snagged by Bailey and fell harshly to the ground. So close to the antidote. "Not on my fucking watch, you bitch!" Bailey screamed, pulling her towards her. Jason stood tall, recovering from his attack. But he was hit again by Jacob with a kick in the back. It only made him jolt forward slightly, as he then turned round to meet eye contact with Jacob with his fists up. "Oh. So, you want to play, huh?" He smiled, putting up his hands "Let's play then, Jacob" Just like that, Jason swung his hand, hitting Jacob right in the face. He stumbled back slightly and winced in pain. But he shook it off and put his hands back up. "You hit like a girl!" Jacob smiled as he then forcefully hit Jason right in the face. The pain seemed throughout his hand. It hurt like hell. But Jacob felt strong, watching Jason fall on his back. But they then had bigger problems. The candles. They fell like dominos onto the floor. But did they notice? No, they did not. Jason stance himself and wiped the blood off his lip with his sleeve. He looked up to Jacob and laughed in a cackle. "That all you got?" Terry was on top of Shea, punching him hard. But she was also met with a fist hitting her face. It made her fall to the side weakly on her back. Just then, Shea jumped on top, wrapping his two hands around her neck, and began choking her. "Rapha!!!" Ashley called after her through her gag. She then spat it out "Holt! You must cut me free! Let me get some action!" "I think we have bigger problems, Ashley" Boyle said, now free from his ropes, and pointed at the candles burning the carpet and spreading like a disease. "We can't stay in here. This building is going to catch that in no time and burn" Holt replied. Amanda was turned on her back, pinned down by Bailey. "You think you can just save the day again!?" She laughed "I've beat you once, I can do it fucking again!" Amanda's eyes widened as she saw her draw out her signature knife. Bailey threw her hand down, but Amanda caught her arm with her free hand. It was ever so close to her chest. But Bailey gritted her teeth and used all her strength to pull it down. "I want you DEAD SANTIAGO!" She screamed, "NO LONGER WILL YOU RUIN MY LIFE WITH JACOB!" Amanda squeezed her eyes shut and groaned through her pain. All her strength pushing upwards. The knife drew closer to her chest... "Say goodbye forever, Amanda-" Bailey was cut off by Jacob whacking her across the head with the metal candle stand. "Jacob!" Amanda smiled with glee as she took his hand and stood tall "Ames, we need to get out! This building is going to burn!"

Amanda looked behind and saw flames now nearly everywhere. It burned the floor and grew to the ceiling. It made her mouth drop with fear. She then looked back to Jacob. "I need that antidote!" "It's alright! Grab that and I'll deal with the other-" Suddenly an arm gripped Jacob's neck and slammed him to the ground. Jason stood tall, panting, grinning. "Jacob!!" Amanda called after him. But she looked at Jason who had now made eye contact. She panicked and turned around to lift the antidote. But it was no longer the case. "Looking for something, Amanda?" A voice called. She turned back round to see Bailey standing holding the glass tube in between her fingers. Blood trickled down her dark face as bright flames behind her began to grow. "Just give me its Bailey and let us go!" Amanda shouted. "Aww... You really think it's that easy?" She pouted with a childish voice "You think life is so fucking easy! Don't you!?" "I don't, Bailey! I don't!" Amanda yelled through the flames "I know you are hurting! I know what you have been through is tough!" Amanda then softened her voice 'It wasn't your fault, Bailey. She still loves you!" Bailey's eyes widened. It was like her anger drained. She was talking about her Mom. Memories of her cradling her Mom in her own pool of blood flashed in her mind. The howling cry of her Dad echoed in her head. All the hate and screaming played in her head like a tape. It wasn't her fault. Her death wasn't her fault. "Bailey..." Amanda said, now taking careful steps. "Don't do this. You are just hurting..." She continued to walk towards her "The reason why you want Jacob so bad, was because he only understood you. He was your only friend..." Amanda then stopped in front of her "You don't have to fight like this. This can all end. Bailey. Your Mom will be proud" For once, Amanda's words made Bailey daze out, soak in her own memories of her Mom. Her smile, her blue eyes, and her beautiful blonde hair. She loved her. She missed her. Tears fell down her cheeks. "No..." She mumbled "NO!" And just like that Bailey was back to her insane self. Ready to swing a hit at Amanda. But Amanda kicked her arm where she held the antidote. Watching it fall to the ground and roll away. "YOU HAVE NO RIGHT TO SPEAK ABOUT HER!" Bailey screamed through her tears, tearing out her knife "I LOVED HER AND IT WAS ALL MY FAULT! BUT NO ONE CARED! I ONLY HAD JACOB! BUT HE GOT TAKEN AWAY BY SOME NERD!" She kicked Amanda in the stomach, pushing out all the air in her lungs and making her fold like a piece of paper. "I FINALLY FOUND HIM AFTER YEARS OF TRAINING IN THE POLICE ACADEMY. BUT YOU TOOK THAT AWAY AGAIN! YOU TOOK THAT AWAY!" She then pinned her down to the ground, held up her knife ever so high, and held it in place "BUT NO LONGER WILL THAT HAPPEN! NO FUCKING MORE!" Amanda looked next to her and grabbed the metal stand as Bailey pulled down the knife. Amanda swung the stand across her head in a smack. Her heart stopped. The knife fell next to her, and Bailey's eyes rolled to the back of her head.

She flopped weakly to the side, like a dead body. Terry scratched at Shea's hands, losing her breath ever so quickly. Her eyes began to be smuggled with blackness. She was passing out, watching the house go dark. But a sudden feeling of air ran down into her lungs. She was breathing. She opened her eyes clearly to see Ashley with a mini pistol in her hand. Panting and shea on the floor groaning. "That is adorable, where did you get that?" "I'll explain later! Right now? This building is about to burn, we need to get out! Fast!" Ashley took her hand and pulled her out, where everyone else was running. "Amanda! We need to go!" Terry shouted behind her. "I'm behind you!" she said, getting up. But wait. The antidote. Where was it? Jacob on the other hand still had his battle. Jason held him in a headlock, now with a gun to his head. "YOU MADE A BAD MISTAKE PERALTA!" He said, digging in the muzzle into the side of his head "NOW YOU WILL REGRET IT ALL!" "You keep forgetting I'm a cop!" Jacob headbutted him backward, making Jason groan and grab his nose, and just like that, how easy it was, Jacob grabbed the gun and pointed it at him. "Get up," he said sternly. Jason held up both hands and stood up slowly, blood trickling down his chin. "You could've stayed out of this! You could've had a normal life! Why!?" "I WAS ALONE!" He screamed "I LOST EVERY-THING! I LOST A FAMILY! A WIFE! BUT YOU WOULDN'T FUCKING UNDERSTAND!" He paused. Looking down "I lost a mother...But you wouldn't understand. I NEEDED AMANDA! I NEEDED A BABY! AND YOU TOOK IT ALL!" Jason charged after Jacob, but he took a quick turn. Jacob was now sharper with his reflex as being better now. Feeling stronger. He took his right leg and kicked him dead center in the chest, making him trip over into the open fireplace. Yeah. That's right. He began to burn. "Jacob! Over here!" Charles called through the flames that were now everywhere. He could see him standing at the door waving his hand. Jacob tried to look for Amanda. But the flames were too bright, suffocating his lungs now. He couldn't see anything bar orange and thick smoke. She must already be outside. Jacob covered his mouth, dodging past all the fire as best as possible. His head began to sweat. It was a living oven. Jacob heard the fire crackle and the wood fall in some places. But he ran to the door, bursting through the cold, damp, raining air, hitting his face. He didn't care. It felt amazing. Jacob hit hard onto his knees bending over and coughing. Behind him, Charles picked him up. Escorting him further away from the building where everyone else is, just watching the building burn. They were all covered in smoke. Mostly Jacob. "Jacob!? Are you alright?" Terry asked, taking his shoulder. Jacob managed to talk in between coughing "Yeah-" He snagged a cough again "I'm fine" He stood tall and looked at everyone. Holt, Ashley, Scully, Terry, Hitchcock, Charles, and Terry all stood with smokey faces and all coughing, drenched in the rain. But one person was missing. Amanda. Amanda wasn't outside like he thought. "Wait!?" he started to look about "Where is Amanda!?" Terry then looked behind her "She said she was right behind me!? I- I could've sworn She was behind me!" Jacob then began to shake with fear and turned back around to the building now crumbling away. Burning. "Amanda is still in there... "

Chapter 17: Departure

Bailey, 12 years old, sat in her room, just lying in her bed at night. Usually, she liked to think a lot at night, while trying to sleep. All wrapped up and eyes just dazed at the ceiling. Some of the thoughts at night were magical, Warm, and happy. She liked to look at how her day went. Smile or maybe laugh. But this night was different. Her head was no longer filled with childish smiles, cuddling memories, or anything with blazing sunshine and rainbows. Instead, she drowned in her own tears. Her head became what was darker than night. Thoughts turned into nightmares and memories flipped into trauma. That smile no longer made her happy. Those eyes no longer made her feel welcome. But now alone... Her mother. She missed her dearly. Her death was not predicted, but not saved. That night, Bailey held her. Her heart was something beyond a beating drum as she watched the blood drool out of her like a waterfall. It was something she couldn't forget. So much happened at that very moment. The robber got away. Jason cried in his bedroom. And her mother took her last breath. "Mom!" She cried out in tears, touching her face "Mom! Stay with me o-okay!? Stay WITH ME!" she screamed, as she watched her slowly take her last breaths. But she remembers, right before she left her. Her blue eyes looked right into Baileys. She froze as tears slid down her cheek, just looking at her Mom go pale. Rachel lifted her hand, tucked her daughter's hair behind her ear, and softened her eyes. Whispering her last words. "You'll make me so proud, Tay. I just know it" Although they didn't slide out so easily.

You can hear the hurt in her voice and the pain. But she left smiling. Those thoughts at night made Bailey choke in her own sadness. She cried herself to sleep silently. The pain still stung ever so hard, even though 4 months have passed. It still hurt. Her favorite thing to cuddle at night was her teddy, snuffles. That stuffed animal meant more to her than her father. It was her only friend at that point. Suddenly Bailey's door opened. Her heart skipped a beat as she threw her body to the other side of her bed and began to sleep. Fearful that it might have been her Dad. "Bailey...?" A young voice called out to her. She slowly moved her head to look behind her. It was Jason. Dressed in all blue pajamas and holding a blanket. He was rubbing his eye, looking at his only older sister. "Why aren't you in bed?" Bailey hissed as she then sat up on her bed. "I can't sleep..." He replied, with a childish pouted lip. "Mr. Nightlight broke again" Bailey rolled her eyes and slammed her body back down onto her bed. "Well," She huffed "That's not my problem. Go get Dad or something." Jason then shuffled his feet closer to her bed and innocently replied.

"He's sleeping on the sofa again," Bailey looked forward to where her window was, curtains still open. The stars and glow of the moon reflected in her eyes. She knew exactly that her Dad was yet again passed out on the sofa. Probably bombarded with bottles of drink. Suddenly her bed sank slightly as she felt Jason climb on top. "Can I sleep here? I promise I'll be good," She listened to his young innocent voice and gave in. She secretly kind of liked the extra company. "Fine! But you better not annoy me, or I'll never let you back in. Okay?" "Okay" He smiled affectionately and immediately made himself comfy underneath the covers. Bailey kept her eyes peeled out of her window. Silence swallowed the room, and she felt her baby brother, Jason, at only 5 years old, being restless. "Tay?" he asked. "What?" She replied, sounding slightly bitter. "Why were you crying?" Bailey froze. It's funny how small kids can be so confident and honest about things. They can be so curious about such small actions, feelings, or words. Bailey sniffed and inhaled and hugged her teddy, Snuffles, tighter. "You won't understand," she said while exhaling. Accidentally letting a tear slip out. "Oh," he then sat up on her bed and started fidgeting with his blanket "Mommy always sang a song when I cried," Bailey's heart broke to those words. Her brother was so innocent. He hadn't talked about her in a while since then. But it made her break down silently again. But she knows the song, her mother's soothing voice also sung to her. The memory made her smile. Bailey then sat up along with Jason and looked at him. "Is that right?" "Yeah, she was really good at it," he said smiling. But just then it started to die down like a dying candle. His warm happiness turned into a frown. He looked down at his blanket, cotton soft and grey, and sighed. "I miss her..." Bailey looked down at her covers as well. She felt his pain. For a little boy so young, it wasn't right for him to feel this way. He should be happy. As should Bailey. But the family was broken. She felt lost. Alone. Weak. The small stuffed bear, material so ruffled and crude, sat next to her. She grabbed it, stroking its matted coated fabric, and traced her finger over its brown marbled eye. "I know..." She paused "I miss her too" "Does Daddy?" Bailey looked at Jason deeply. She didn't know about him. Bailey didn't even want to think about him. He was no longer the person she remembered. All he did was sit on the couch and drink his worries away. Bailey was smart enough to know what was going on.

She was switched on. But she didn't want Jason to worry about him or feel scared of the only person who was now their parent. So, she whisked the subject away "How about we treat ourselves tonight?" she asked with a welcoming smile. Jason's eyes gleamed "Like what?" "Anything, anything you want! You know the little corner shop down the street?" "That scary street...?" "Here" She handed him her teddy "This is Snuffles, the best protector in the world. Hold onto him tightly and I promise, nothing will go wrong." Jason took him slowly, feeling his material. "Promise?" he asked. "Promise" she then hopped out of bed and lifted him off "When we go out here, we have to be quiet, okay? Don't

want Daddy to know" "Okay!" She took his hand and took him carefully out of her room and into where her Dad sat, passed out on the sofa. He was out of it. TV was turned static, and bottles lay everywhere.
Bailey looked down at Jason who held Snuffles tightly in one arm and
the other held her hand. Bailey placed her finger on her lips to tell him
to be quiet. She let go of his small baby hand and tip-toed over to her
Dad. His snoring became louder in her ears. Her heart thumped rapid-
ly. She looked for his wallet. Bailey noticed the shape-like object, buried
into his jeans. Just 10 dollars. That's all she needed. Bailey dinged her
fingers carefully and timidly took out his wallet. She was halfway there.
Suddenly her Dad stopped snoring and moved his head. She was a deer
froze at the sight of headlights. Her blood turned ice cold and her heart
stopped. But he drunkenly licked his lips and moved his head to the
other side, still passed out, and continued to snore. Bailey sighed with
such heavy relief. She took his wallet, stole ten dollars, and walked back
to Jason. "Are we doing bad?" He whispered as she took him outside.
Bailey looked up to the sky and remembered her Mom's words about
making her proud. Maybe some other time she will... "No..." She smiled
"She is okay with this" Bailey took his hand and walked down the street
with Jason, holding onto Snuffles tightly.

Jacobs's heart raced faster than the spinning wheels of a car. His fear
pulsed through his body and Jacob could feel the thump of his heart
throbbing in his ear. Amanda was still within those lioness flames.
Roaring and dancing as they crumble away the once-called beach
house. "Amanda is still in there..." He said, almost shivering at his own
words. He then jumped to his feet and raced to the house, sprinting towards the burning door. The squad behind called after him.

   "Jacob! Wait!" Charles called out, running out after him but was
tugged back by Terry. "You can't go in there!" he spun Charles around
"It's way too dangerous!" "But Jacob-" "He'll be okay!" Terry replied.

Charles gave up and relaxed his body. His eyes reflected in the flames as he watched with contempt. Jacob bolted inside, immediately being hit by a pool of smoke, sliding down his throat and choking him. It was almost like it was strangling his lungs. He began to cough, putting his hand up to cover some of the light and smoke attacking his eyes. The heat made him sweat and burn up, almost feel like he was cooking up like a chicken. But he couldn't see Amanda anywhere among the bold orange flames. Flames. Yellow and orange. That's all he could see. "Amanda!?" He called out, then choking on what he inhaled "A-" He coughed "Amanda!? Where are you!?"

Amanda was on her hands and knees, searching for the antidote. She saw it fall out of Bailey's hands and roll into the bliss. Her lungs felt tight as she continued to cough from the smoke colliding inside of her. She couldn't see a thing. The black smoke burned her eyes, and the flames were too bright. She patted her hand on the floor, just hoping to see or feel the antidote somewhere. She needed that so badly. She could die. She never knew how, but from Bailey's words. It ended in death, and she believed it. She continued to crawl like a baby on the floor, just patting the floor. Amanda's face was sweating in the heat, she could feel the flames grow larger around her. Suddenly. Amanda's head felt like someone was compressing a clamp on her brain and tightening it. Squeezing it. The pain was something no one can describe. She screamed in agony, placing her two hands on her head like it would help it stop. This was stage four. "AAAHHH" She yelled in pain on the floor, feeling her body warm up faster. "Make it stop! Make it stop!!" Tears slipped down her face. But she barely noticed. Her head felt like it was about to go to mush. Like a thousand tiny little swords surrounding it, that's how it felt. It was worse than just a normal headache. It made her body stop in shock, lying on the floor in agony. Amanda was coughing, losing her sight. Smoke surrounded her and flames grew around her. But something among the flames she could hear her name being called. "Ames!?" She heard again "Amanda!? Call out to me! Ames!" It was Jacob's voice. It gave her hope. She tried to sit up, but she couldn't. Her body began to shut down. Her eyelids became weak, and her voice was snatched. The only thing coming out of her was painful coughs. Jacob held his arm up higher, blocking the light. He covered his mouth with his free hand. Spitting and coughing. The black smoke collided within inside. He could feel it sting his eyes, throat, and lungs. But his biggest concern was Amanda. He couldn't see a thing. His eyes could no longer recognize the beach house. Now it was just a pool of flames.

Hot, burning flames. But suddenly his eyes caught upon something odd further in the distance. Something lying on the floor. Amanda. "Ames!" Jacob shouted, not caring that the smoke slid down his throat. Amanda lay on the floor holding her ears shut, groaning in agony. Jacob fell to his knees and placed her on her back, holding her head. "Amanda, what's wrong!? Talk to me!" But the only response she gave back was continued small groans of pain and coughing. Her face was covered in black soot. Her hands were covered too. Her face was pale but glazed with her own sweat. Jacob couldn't see her like this. It hurt him. "It's called stage four, dumbass! You're too fucking late!" He heard a voice call. Jacob squinted his eyes and looked up. There, stood Jason. His clothes were burnt. Some of his hair was gone and his arm was bubbled with blisters. Jacob almost thought he killed him. Watching him fall backwards into the fireplace not long ago. "Where is the antidote!?" Jacob called out. Jason laughed, placing his hand on his chest, and cackled like a hyena. "Somewhere among these lioness flames, Jacoby!" He laughed again "It's gone! Nowhere to be seen!" Jacob's eyebrows knitted together in a worry. He looked down at Amanda who still struggled in pain. "But I will make an offer... Jacob" Jason continued. He then slid his burnt fingers into the deep right-hand side of his pocket and lifted out a small glass tube. Another antidote. "Now, mind you, Jacob. I like to be prepared for a lot of things..." He smiled, holding the antidote high in between his index finger and thumb "I'll give you an offer" His crooked smile stretched. "I give this to your little Ames, and she will live, but!" He pulled out a grin and a laugh again "Princess will belong to me" "She doesn't belong to anyone. "He replied, not in a repulsive way. But calming. "She is her own person but will never be taken by you." "Oh really?" Jason ran his hand through his hair. "Fine then. Take the hard way" He then threw the antidote to the floor and crushed it with his shoe. Listening to the tiny glass tube shatter into little shards. Jacob reached out his hand, like he would've caught it in time, but froze as he watched it being demolished. "No..." Jacob whispered to himself "No.." The only second one who could reach was gone. Sure. The first antidote is still within the house. But impossible to find. Jason laughed. "Whoopsie" He smiled "Fingers slipped..."

Jacob looked down to Amanda whose eyes seemed relaxed, her arms were by her side and her chest rose slowly but surely. Jacob's mind became suspicious. Unsure. Scared. "Amanda?' She shook her face slightly "Ames!?" But her weak, covered face was still. Not reacting to his touch. Suddenly Jacob watched a small amount of blood drip out of her right nostril. But that's not the only thing that made him shiver. A sound of a trigger being pulled back, pulsed and echoed in his ear. "If I can't have her..." Jacob looked up and saw Jason pointing a gun at her. But Jacob did nothing but hold onto her tighter, as he pierced his eyes on the front view of the muzzle. "Then no one can." Jacob squinted and buried his head into Amanda. For some reason, he never thought to attack at that very second or take her away to safety. Instead. Jacob would rather take the hit. He will take it any day over Amanda. But there she was, unconscious in his warm arms. Holding onto her tightly. BANG The sound echoed in the rain. The gang outside all froze in horror, faces and hair soaked and curled like rotten seaweed. Their face glowed from the fire. All eyes were wide, and mouths were shut. They had no clue as to what happened. But their soul left their body in fear. But Jacob opened his squinted eyes. Nothing hit him or hurt him. Jacob slowly lifted his head and saw Bailey standing in front of them. Her back was turned to Jacob lying on the floor with Amanda. But everything went slow. Jason's devilish grin flipped into something that looked more than fear. Regret. His eyes went wider than golf balls and his mouth swung open. The pistol slowly slid out of his blistered hand and fell harshly to the ground. Bailey took the hit. Right in the chest. Bailey placed her hand over her wound and fell forward into Jason's arms. "BAILEY!" He screamed while catching her "NO! TAY!" Jason fell to his knees while cradling her as she kept her eyes facing the front. The fire grew, the rain got heavier, and the atmosphere was dead. Jason cried in fear, placing his hand over her chest and stroking her face. "Bailey, no! This can't be happening!" "Jason..." She managed out with a smile she had never broken out before. A genuine smile. "Don't waste your tears" "I can't lose you! W-we must get you out-" "Jason" She repeated calmly "Stop" "Why!?" He sobbed "Why did you do it!!?" Bailey didn't answer Jason. Instead, she looked across to Jacob. She smiled, but it hurt. A tear slipped down her dirty face, leaving a clear clean line, and breathed deeply. She weakly put her hand out and opened her palm. An antidote was revealed. She was the one who found it.

Jacob looked into her eyes with such sorrow. But Bailey smiled. He reached over and grabbed it with caution. "Bailey..." he said, but she cut him off. "I held onto the past, Jacoby..." Thunder roared outside along with the flames. "For so long, I forced something that would have never happened." She laughed, but out of pity "I never felt loved. But I did have one person who did" She then looked above at the burning ceiling, like she could see who she was thinking of above. "But when she left me... You were the only person who made me feel safe, Jacob" She then looked at him again "I was afraid to lose that..." Bailey then looked at Amanda who was still unconscious and gazed at the burning fire around. She took a breath again. "But I'm not afraid anymore. But I want you to make someone else feel the same. Make them feel like they have someone." She examined Amanda one last time "Cause I know that, that person will be lucky. Lucky enough to have that love." Jacob couldn't believe what she was saying. He didn't know what changed her. But all the hate, all the anger. Was out of pain. Neglect. It made him feel ashamed of their past. Bailey changed. She changed right after she had that flashback of her mother's words to her while she was knocked out. She realized how much pain she was holding in. How much she disappointed her mother. How much it can hurt to lose a loved one. "Go," She said to him "Take her out of here, show her what I always wanted. Okay?" Jacob paused, looking into her blue eyes. Those memories now hurt. That teenage smile he gave her when Jacob made a stupid joke. Or their locker engraved with their initials. He remembered their first kiss under the bleachers in school. Their first date. Movie nights. That was the Bailey who he liked. But he remembered her face when it was over between them. She needed him. Bailey needed someone who she knew, loved her. Those memories didn't anger him no more. It hurt him. Broke him. Jacob choked "I will," He lifted Amanda and broke his way through the flames, dodging every falling plank. Every heap of smoke and fire. He looked down at Amanda who's color was now white. The small blood on her nose was dry. But she was out cold. Jacob wanted to look behind him. But he already made it outside. Hearing everyone run to him with fear. Bailey looked at Jason. "Jason" She smiled and cupped his face "You were always my priority. My baby bro" Jason laughed and cuddled his face into her hand deeper and let his tears go loose. "But it's time to let those wounds heal. Forget the past. Because those scars heal, Jason. They fade over time..." She paused "You can't change the past." She then glanced down at her very own spilling wound. It terrified her. But she kept a brave face on and looked back up to her brother.

"But you can change who you are today." "I can't lose you, Bailey! I can't!" he stressed through his tears "I've lost everything!" "No. We will be looking over it. Like she always did" "Why did you do it!? You didn't have to sacrifice yourself for them!!! You didn't!!!" "One day, you will understand" Bailey began to close her eyes, softening her words "You will make me proud, Jason. I just know it" And just like that. Her hand went weak on his face, slowly dropping and her eyes became heavier than they seemed. Jason whispered her name, hoping she would respond. But his hope was gone. He howled in a cry. Cradling his own sister in his arms. Wailing. Repeating wailing. He took his pistol on the floor and stood to his feet. He screamed out in anger and shot several rounds into the ceiling out of rage. His face was red, his eyes were glossy, and his heart was broken. Suddenly a hand rested on his shoulder. Shea. He gave him a pity smile. Jason rested his arm and lowered the gun. Sobbing. And fell to his knees.

"There he is!" Terry called out as she could see Jacob, face covered with black smoke, carrying Amanda and running out. He immediately fell to his knees, still holding onto Amanda. He lay her down gently onto the soaked ground where raindrops bounced and took out the antidote. He cried. Quietly though, as he forced the liquid into her mouth. He watched her patiently. Seconds felt like minutes and minutes felt like hours. He just waited for a reaction. The squad gathered around them. All drenched, but not caring. They all looked down at Amanda and Jacob who was now calling her name. "Amanda?" He stroked her wet hair "Come on, get up" No response. "She saved us, Ames" Jacob laughed in a cry "She saved us!" But Amanda lay still. Black smoke now slowly dripping off her face as the rain was washing it away slightly. "But she is free," He looked up to the sky, squinting as God's shower hit his face "She was just hurt...." Jacob shot his head back down "She was just alone..." he inhaled "Please, wake up Ames..." Jacob watched her like a hawk, waiting seconds. Until a sudden cough echoed. Amanda folded over and began to cough, choking on the remaining smoke within her. "Amanda!!" Jacob hugged her immediately, putting his hand over her head and holding onto her tight. He couldn't help but cry, out of everything that had happened. "Jacob" She croaked "We made it?" She asked, parting their hug. "We made it" He smiled "We are okay," Amanda gave him a warm smile, grabbing his face and kissing him affectionately. Suddenly several gunshots echoed within the house. Startling the entire squad. Amanda got to her feet, weakly, as did Jacob. They all stood in a group, watching the beach house burn and crumble into simply nothing. It glowed upon their faces with fiery oranges and sunburned yellows, all standing in silence. The only sounds to hear were the drumming rain and the crackle of the fire. It was something that made them all go silent. Even Jacob. Knowing Bailey was gone. Bold, blue, red lights flicked behind them, casting the squad's silhouette. They heard the crying sirens of the police cars but didn't dare to withdraw their eyes from the building. It snatched their attention. Multiple cops, firefighters, and doctors came rushing out of cars. Some took some of the squad, such as Ashley, Boyle, Terry, Charles, Scully, Hitchcock and Amanda. All being pulled away, placed to get medical checkups. Mostly Amanda. Terry got pulled away with Charles to explain the whole story. But Jacob was left standing right in front of the building, watching the firefighters try to choke out the fire. His mind was lost within there. He couldn't wipe Bailey's sorrowful eyes. Those eyes were just always in pain. Holt stood next to him, silently. "She was in pain," Jacob finally spoke. Holt looked down at him, spectating every emotion on his face, and looked back at the building. Hands behind his back. "Many people bundle their fears, traumas, and pain into a ball and Bury it deep. Exchanging it for hate. Do you know why, Peralta?" Jacob looked at him with no words. But Holt knew that he wanted the answer. He continued "It's because they rather block that. Put on a mask and blame everyone else for their pain, because they can't handle it on their own. They rather look brave, than let people see what is hurting within." Jacob nodded his head in response. The night was cold. He was cold. Small drips of rain ran down his face and cried out of his hair like tears. But not once did he shiver. "Excuse me, officer," A policeman came up to Jacob. "What's up?" "We were informed there would be three more people within the building. But the news is negative, sir. There was no sign of anyone in the building" Jacob investigated the, once standing, building. It was now all blackened wooden planks. Half crumbled to the ground. "Thank you, officer. That will be all," Suddenly Jacob felt something warm wrap around him. Behind, Amanda placed a blanket over him and stood next to Jacob. Looking at what he was. "You okay, Jacob?" she asked, concerned for him. He paused, then looked at her. "Of course," He smiled "I've got you," He placed his arm over her and began to walk away. He wanted Amanda to be safe. She was safe, of course. But knowing that Jason or Shea weren't found in the building, still unsettled him. But it was all over. Everything was going to be okay. 'Cause he had Amanda...

Don't miss out!

Visit the website below and you can sign up to receive emails whenever M.J. MOON publishes a new book. There's no charge and no obligation.

https://books2read.com/r/B-A-LBAOB-QMBLD

BOOKS 2 READ

Connecting independent readers to independent writers.

Also by M.J. MOON

Nothing More Than A Puppet

About the Author

M.J. Moon is a passionate writer dedicated to crafting stories that inspire and captivate young hearts. With a love for children's literature and a knack for weaving tales of wonder, M.J. Moon creates imaginative worlds where characters embark on unforgettable adventures.

Born with a vivid imagination and a belief in the magic of storytelling, M.J. Moon's writing reflects a deep appreciation for the innocence and curiosity of childhood. From whimsical picture books that spark laughter to heartfelt short novels that explore themes of courage and friendship, each story is crafted with care and a touch of enchantment.

When not immersed in the world of words, M.J. Moon enjoys exploring nature, seeking inspiration from the beauty of the outdoors. Whether through playful rhymes or poignant narratives, M.J. Moon's writing aims to leave a lasting impression, encouraging young readers to dream big and embrace the joy of reading.

About the Publisher

www.ingramcontent.com/pod-product-compliance
Lightning Source LLC
Chambersburg PA
CBHW061242170626
46809CB00007B/2788